DEADLY MEETING

She pulled up at a stop sign and glanced in the rearview mirror. Adrenaline shot through her at the sight of a man's face staring back at her.

"I have a knife, so don't scream," he said softly, right into her ear.

She shook her head, indicating she wouldn't.

The soft voice continued: "Turn right here and just drive till I tell you where to turn."

The knife was at her throat now; she could feel the thin blade. It was a woman's worst nightmare coming true.

DEATH CLAIM

Joan Banks

CHARTER BOOKS, NEW YORK

DEATH CLAIM

A Charter Book/published by arrangement with
the author

PRINTING HISTORY
Charter edition/July 1988

ISBN: 1-55773-049-0

Charter Books are published by The Berkley Publishing Group,
200 Madison Avenue, New York, New York 10016.

PRINTED IN THE UNITED STATES OF AMERICA

10 9 8 7 6 5 4 3 2 1

To
Michael, Betsy, John,
Charlotte and Don,
and to
Margaret Palmer,
where it all began

PROLOGUE

The girl darts from between parked cars on the narrow, apartment-lined street. He slams on the brakes, skidding, and the world appears to him in slow motion as the body lifts into the air and disappears soundlessly. An eternal second. Then time careens forward again as he jams his foot onto the accelerator and finds himself speeding away from the scene. Only the prickly sweat on his temples keeps him in touch with what he just witnessed, what he just did.

I

"Claims. Lora speaking."

A woman's voice at the other end of the line babbled something unintelligible. Lora Montgomery handled all the calls coming in from New York State, but she still had trouble understanding the accent at times. To be honest, the difficulty wasn't one-sided. She didn't think she had picked up much of a Texas drawl from her ten years in Dallas, but sometimes her New York callers accused her of sounding just like Lady Bird.

"I beg your pardon," she said into her headset, "Will you repeat that please?"

"I need to report that my car has been stolen," the woman said again, more slowly this time.

"Hold on a moment and I'll take your report as soon as I get a screen on my computer." She punched in the appropriate code on her keyboard to pull up the form for stolen cars. When it appeared, she asked routinely, "What's your member number please?"

"Member number?" the woman asked, puzzled.

"It's on your membership card."

"Oh. I'll have to find it. Just hold on a second while I get my purse."

"It's on your policy, too, if you have it there with you," Lora said, her voice trailing off as she realized she was talking to thin air. The woman had already left the phone. Unconsciously, Lora began to twist a strand of her hair as she waited. She glanced at her watch, then at the entrance to the room and the hallway beyond. If Brad Conroy went by on his way to the staff room, she would see him. It was a little game she played with herself—trying to get to the staff room at the same time Brad did. It made breaks so much more interesting—something to anticipate each day. She was reminded of junior high school ploys, being in the right place at the right time, when the "man" of the hour, who changed almost weekly, sauntered by, usually unaware of her interest.

Brad was the personnel manager—unmarried, good-looking, successful. Unfortunately he was also young, about thirty, she would guess. Not that the age difference bothered her too much. She was thirty-eight, with warm brown eyes—doelike when she wore a touch of mascara—and soft, shoulder-length brown hair, feathered casually back from her face because she had read somewhere that sweeping the hair back was more youthful—a face largely untouched by age in any bad sort of way, at least to a noncritical observer. To Lora, though, her face had changed a lot, just in the past year. It had softened, with little pillows of flesh where there had never been any before. Would she soon be jowly? she wondered, as she gazed in the mirror each morning, her face puffy from sleep, wrinkles from the bedclothes etched into her skin. She noticed the skin even fled before her fingers when she applied makeup now, refusing to stay taut where it should. Yes, she felt she could no longer be particular about details such as age differences.

The caller returned to the phone and gave Lora the information she needed. When Lora had punched it in, the video display terminal flashed the policy information. She went through her usual routine efficiently, verifying the woman's address and phone number.

"When did this happen?" she asked.

"You mean the car?"

"Yes," she said patiently, "the car. When was it stolen?"

"I don't know exactly, except sometime today when I was at work." The floodgate opened and the woman began to pour out her story, her reticence gone. "You see, I take the bus to work because parking is such a hassle. My boyfriend doesn't think I even need a car since I don't drive it to work. Well, anyway, when I got home today the car was gone from its parking place. I came home early because I quit my job. I was a waitress, and you wouldn't believe how hard it was. You know, standing on your feet all day, and the b.s. you have to take from pèople—''

''I can imagine,'' Lora broke in sympathetically. ''Well, have you reported it—about the car—to the police?'' she asked, directing the conversation back to the subject, feeling a little guilty about not letting the woman ramble on.

''Uh . . . no.'' The woman hesitated. ''Do I have to do that?'' she asked, reverting to her timid manner.

''Well, yes, I'm afraid so. They might be able to locate it. Besides, it's company policy. To make a claim, there has to be a police report. Why don't you go ahead and do that, then call me back?''

''Okay,'' she said reluctantly, ''if you're sure I have to.''

''Yes, I'm sure. What I need is the precinct number of the police station where you report it, the case number, and the name of the officer you talk to.''

''Wait a minute, let me get a pencil and paper.''

Lora wondered how many times a week she heard that sentence, or, ''Wait, my pen won't write.''

She began to fiddle with her hair again while she waited, glancing at the hallway. There was Brad going toward the staff room. Hurry, she willed the caller, who returned to the phone at that moment.

''Okay, I found something to write on, a napkin,'' the caller said, giggling self-consciously.

Lora repeated the information she needed. Then she said, ''I'll leave your file open while I wait to hear from you, okay?''

''Yes. I'll call you back. But I guess it might be too late today, by the time I make the report and everything. Well, I don't know, there might be time, but—''

"Tomorrow will be fine."

"Well—thanks for taking your time with me and helping me and all. I was kind of wondering if I should've quit my job, and then this happened and everything—"

"I'm sure everything will turn out okay, and I'll expect your call tomorrow."

"Okay, well, bye then."

"Good-bye." And thank goodness. There was still time to catch Brad on break. She started to take off her headset and switch the calls to another line, but she was too late. Another call.

Disappointed, she answered. "Claims. Lora speaking."

2

Shera Johnson was a law-abiding citizen. The most contact she'd had with the police was a ticket left on her car by a meter maid in the town where she had grown up. But since parking fines were paid by simply putting the money in the ticket, which was an envelope, and depositing it in a metal box attached to a meter, even that hadn't given her any reason to visit a police station.

Now she found herself on the steps to the two-story brownstone precinct house in her neighborhood. She had passed it many times, feeling vaguely more secure, knowing it was just a few blocks from her apartment, but she had never anticipated going in. She had tried to avoid it now, by calling, but the officer had told her she had to report an incident in person, that he would send someone over. No, she'd insisted, she would come to the police station. She knew, with superstitious certainty, that if the police came to the apartment, her boyfriend Tony would reappear at the same time. That's the way things worked in life. And she didn't need that kind of complication.

She climbed the granite steps, puddled out in the middle from long use, and went in the heavy double doors, struggling against their weight. The high-ceilinged, institutional green interior looked familiar, as if she had seen it on television. Two policemen stood talking at one side of a high desk that faced her; another was behind it. An old woman sat bolt upright, but with her eyes closed, on an oak bench against a wall. The shopping cart in front of her was loaded with parcels.

Shera approached the desk timorously. The men didn't acknowledge her presence, so finally she said, "Pardon m-me." Her voice broke as she said it, so she cleared her throat and began again. "Pardon me, but I n-need to report a st-stolen car."

All three of the policemen turned to look at her as if she'd suddenly become visible, and she shrank back a step or two, feeling embarrassed by their attention. She unconsciously pulled at the seams of her jeans, which were too tight, and as she did, the strap of her bag fell off her shoulder and dropped to the wooden floor with a thump. She bent over to pick it up and felt some of the threads in her jeans's seam snap.

When her head bobbed up again over the top of the desk, the officer behind it said, "You say your car was stolen?"

Shera nodded.

"Just go have a seat over there and I'll get someone in here to help you." He dipped his head toward the bench where the old woman sat.

Shera walked over and sat down next to the woman, who still appeared to be dozing, being careful not to disturb her. The officers went back to their discussion, and shortly a florid-faced officer appeared from down a hallway and spoke to the desk man, then approached Shera. She rose to meet him.

"I'm Detective Maddox. If you'll just come with me . . ." he said, and led her back the way he'd come.

They turned into a room crammed with half a dozen vintage wooden desks, twice as many green metal file cabinets, some chairs, and a few people. The officer led her through the maze to his desk and asked her to be seated. Simultaneously, he plopped down with a sigh into his swivel chair and rolled a piece of paper into the typewriter.

"Your name?" he asked.

"Shera Johnson."

"Spell it, please."

She spelled as he typed.

He continued with routine questions, which she answered automatically.

"Make of car?"

"Dodge."

"Year?"

"1973."

"Model?"

She hesitated. "Uh . . . you mean like a Dart?"

"Is it a Dart?"

She nodded. He typed.

"Color?"

"I call it gold, but it's not a metal kind of gold, you know?"

He peered at her intently for a moment, a frown forming, his fingers still hovering over the typewriter keys. "A gold '73 Dart?" he repeated.

What was wrong? she wondered as she nodded in response. What had she said? She began to twist her fingers together.

"Just a minute, young lady. I'll be right back." He got up and left the room.

Maybe she shouldn't have come. But it was too late now; they had her name and address and everything.

Maddox came back with another man behind him. The second man was about forty, six feet tall, with blond hair that appeared to be frosted but was actually streaked with the beginnings of what would someday furnish him with a head of white hair, if he were lucky and didn't lose it first—but time seemed to be against him, because it was beginning to thin on top already. His blue eyes had well-developed squint lines at their corners, giving him a sympathetic look.

"Miss, uh . . ." He glanced at Maddox.

"Johnson," Maddox supplied.

"Miss Johnson, I'm Bill Graham." He extended his hand.

"Now, Miss Johnson, when did you notice your car was missing?" Graham asked as he pulled a chair up from an adjacent desk and straddled it backward.

"Well . . ." Shera fumbled with the clasp on her purse. Her gaze dropped to her lap. "I was at work, and when I got home, it was gone." Why were they looking at her so intently? She didn't want all this attention focused on her. It was just like in school when the teacher would accuse someone of cheating. Even though she hadn't, she would feel guilty, and she always felt she looked guilty, too.

"When did you leave for work?" Graham asked.

"About nine," she said softly.

"I beg your pardon?" he said, not hearing her.

"About nine," she repeated more loudly.

"Where do you work?"

"Well . . . I don't anymore. I quit today."

"Where did you work?" he asked.

She named the small café where she had worked behind the counter.

"We could verify that you were there?"

"Oh, sure. I guess. I mean, I was there, but they may be a little ticked off at me because I quit without any notice. but I'm sure they'd say I was there." It sounded as if he were asking for an alibi. What did she need with an alibi? It was her car that was missing. Did they think she was lying?

"Where did you leave the car?"

She frowned. "Leave it?" Were they trying to trick her?

"I mean, was it in a garage, or what?"

"Oh, no. It was at the curb in front of my apartment house. That's where I always park it."

"Locked?"

She nodded.

"What time did you get home?"

"Well, I guess about three. Like I said, I quit my job today, so I left after the lunch rush; I did give them that." She didn't explain that the reason she had waited was because it was payday, and she hadn't quit till after the manager passed out the paychecks. "Then I cashed my check, and it was probably about three when I got home."

She gripped her purse tighter, remembering the money was still in it, all she had in the world till she found another job, which would have to be soon.

"Could someone have borrowed the car?" Graham asked.

"No," she said quickly. "There's no one." She felt proud not even mentioning Tony. He would be angry enough as it was, if he found out she had gone to the police. She took a deep breath and dared ask, "Is—is there s-something wrong—about my car?"

"Well, Miss Johnson," Graham said, "a gold Dart was seen leaving a hit-and-run accident this morning." He looked intently at her, adding quietly, "A child was killed."

"Oh, migosh, you think maybe I—"

Graham shook his head reassuringly. "Not you. No one got the license number, so unless we find the car . . ." He shrugged, leaving the sentence dangling. "A man was driving, however. A witness did see that. Your missing car kind of fits in."

Yes, it certainly did. And she had the feeling she knew who the man was. It made her feel sick to her stomach.

After she signed a form, the policeman dismissed her and she began to retrace her path to the apartment mechanically, paying no attention to the people on the sidewalks or to the increased traffic in the street signaling the time of the day. She was wrapped up in her own thoughts.

Shera recalled how she had arrived home earlier and noticed that the car wasn't by the curb, where she'd left it. She'd gone up to the apartment unconcerned, assuming Tony borrowed it—he had an extra key—but she found him asleep on the couch.

"Toh-nee," she whined, "where's my car?"

She had to repeat her question to wake him. He sat up,

his movements heavy with the grogginess of afternoon sleep, and wiped his fingers across his heavy dark eyebrows and down his cheeks. "How should I know?" he mumbled, and yawned. "You think I keep my eye on it all the time?"

His tone told Shera she should tread lightly, he was not in the best of moods for being questioned. But she was becoming agitated herself. "Where could it be?"

"Ripped off, probably," he muttered, his hands cradling his head, elbows on his knees. "Oh, God, I feel awful. What time is it, anyway?"

"Ripped off? My car?" her voice was beginning to rise hysterically.

"Why not? In this crummy neighborhood what do you expect? What do you need a car for anyway? You take the bus to work." He still sat there, staring at the floor. He paused, then said softly, "Hell, I don't know what happened to it. I had to go down to the corner for some beer because you didn't buy me any, like I told you, and when I got back it was gone."

"Did you report it?"

He shrugged off her question. "I thought maybe one of your other friends had it."

He knew better than that, that she didn't have any other friends, that she was as much of a loner as he. Why was he being like this? "Well, don't you think we better report it, Tony?" she asked indecisively. She had put her shoulder bag on the couch and was wringing her hands till the knuckles were turning white.

"No," he said, "we won't report it. We're not going to get involved with the cops." He stood up as he spoke. "No way. What do you have in it anyway? A couple of hundred bucks. It's not worth getting the police on our case." The muscle at the corner of his well-shaped, almost feminine mouth began to twitch, and she knew he was getting excited, even though his voice was calm.

"What am I going to do?" she asked, tracking the subtle changes in his face. His pupils had dilated, turning his already dark eyes black.

He took a moment, visibly relaxing, then walked over to her, put one hand up to her face and stroked it reassuringly. In a soft voice completely alien to that of a moment before, he said, "Listen, just trust me, babe. We don't want the cops." He smiled gently at her. "Why don't you just get your uniform off," he added, fingering the front placket which concealed the buttons, "and get comfortable." He drew his fingertips across her breasts, then reached around her and pulled her to him, leaning his face down into the hollow of her neck, kissing it.

She enjoyed the intimacy for a moment, then broke it by saying, "But they could get my car back, maybe." She was near tears now, and her voice had taken on a tinny quality, its whine had become so insistent. "I need my car back; I may need to sell it."

He pulled his head away and looked at her quizzically, his heavy eyebrows drawing toward each other.

She flushed under his scrutiny and looked down to avoid his gaze. "I quit my job today."

"You what?" His voice sounded incredulous.

"I—I quit my job."

"What in the hell did you go and do that for?" His eyes narrowed. "What are you going to live on? I hope to God you don't expect me to set you up here."

"You knew I didn't like it there. I told you I was thinking of quitting."

"Is that the kind of thing we have?" he asked petulantly. "You don't even talk it over with me before you up and do something like quitting?"

"I'm sorry, Tony. I guess I didn't think." She stood before him, shoulders slumped, her head down. She started to turn and walk away, and in a tiny voice asked, "But what about my car? What should I do?"

"God!" he threw both hands up in the air. "Shut up about it, will you?" He slammed his fist against the wall, then turned and grabbed her arm and pulled her up to him. "I can't stand it when I hear you whining all the time," he exhaled through clenched teeth. "You remind me of my mother."

"Please don't hit the wall, Tony, the neighbors . . ." She had gone too far. She knew it before the sentence was finished.

He threw open the door and yelled, "Fuck the neighbors." He glowered back at her. "You better sure as hell have me some beer when and *if* I decide to come back."

"Toh-nee, I'm sorry," he said as she stomped down the stairs. "I didn't mean to make you mad at me." But Tony was already halfway to the ground floor.

Now, after hearing about the hit-and-run, she understood why he hadn't wanted to call the police, why he had been so short-tempered—not that he wasn't often short tempered these days.

She hadn't seen that about him at first, when she met him at the café. He often ate his lunch there. He was a salesman, selling office specialties like pencils and ballpoint pens with name imprints, and she believed he could have sold anything to anyone with his good looks and quixotic appeal—at least to any woman. Men didn't particularly trust him. For women, though, his tousled hair drooping slightly over his forehead, the way he would look up from under those thick eyelashes—sexy but with some curious overlay of innocence—and the strong sense of charmed exclusivity a woman had when she was with him were almost irresistible.

It was a surprise to Shera when Tony began to show an interest in her. She knew all too well that she was plain, with mousy brown hair too fine to hold a style. She wore it long, down to her waist, and pulled it back with a rubber band.

Her weight, too, was a problem; her mother had made her very aware of that, always making comments about how she needed to lose her baby fat. Nagging at her about her weight, then serving dessert with every meal, she'd say, "Because your father expects it." Shera had been glad to get away when she turned eighteen.

She had been lonely until Tony moved into her life—Tony, she thought warmly, Tony who said he liked long hair and a woman with a little meat on her. He always knew just what to say.

Maybe she was getting a little too heavy, she reflected. She'd noticed him watching a woman at the market who was practically skin and bones. Shera unconsciously tugged at her jeans again as she walked along the street.

Their first date had been a blustery autumn afternoon when the wind swept down between the buildings, foretelling the loneliness of winter to come. Tony had come into the café with a gust of cold air, but his smile had warmed up her particular little world. He ordered a cup of coffee and suggested they go to a movie when she got off. She had seen him in there a lot, of course, or she wouldn't have gone out with him.

They had gotten along just fine, even though she'd been

nervous. Tony was just so easy to be with. He wasn't talkative, and she tended to go on and on when she was nervous, but the evening turned out okay. And she felt like a million dollars, just being seen with him.

After the movie he left her at the door of the apartment, without so much as touching her. She had been impressed by what a gentleman he was, and spent the night fantasizing about her wonderful bit of fate. By morning, though, she had decided he probably had a girlfriend who was out of town or something, and was asking herself why he'd been such a gentleman. Was there something wrong with her?

But then he had invited her out again, and this time he had come in afterward, at her invitation. Before she knew what was happening, he was making love to her. It wasn't quite what Shera had anticipated. Not being experienced, she had let him have his way, because he expected it. The truth was Tony was only the second man who had ever kissed her. And Tony didn't stop with a kiss, as the other man had.

She had been reluctant at first. Tony laughingly called her a prude, though not in a mean way, and convinced her that the things he did to her were just part of how he felt toward her.

He awakened something in Shera that she had never felt previously. His touch would make her feel quivery all over. Since she hadn't felt that way before, she thought he had some special quality and worried that if Tony went away, she wouldn't feel that way again.

He moved in—at least he spent the nights there. His clothes were still at his mother's. It was never a big decision for him to live there; he'd just begun to stay over more often.

One day it dawned on her that she was living with someone. She could also trace when things began to change back to that same time period. He no longer treated her as if she were special. The compensation for her was that she felt married—something about the pattern of their lives began to achieve a permanent feeling. And with the married feeling came the other Tony, the one who hit her. Once he had even beat her up. But she didn't have anywhere else to go, and besides, she probably deserved it because she was being so bitchy. That's what he had told her.

Shera occasionally hinted about getting married, but Tony wouldn't talk about it. He said things were fine as they were, so why mess with them. If it ain't broke, don't fix it, he said. He couldn't leave his mother, anyway, he would say. He still had most of his clothes there, at his mother's house, and he went there each morning to dress for work. Shera didn't really understand why, but she had to accept it or lose him. And because Tony was the first person who had ever made her feel special, she accepted it. Even now, even when things were bad—like when he beat on her—she at least knew she was visible to someone.

"Miss Johnson. Yoo-hoo, Miss Johnson." The voice broke into her thoughts from a distance, bringing her back to the present just as she was turning to go up her front steps. She glanced around and saw her landlady hurrying down the block, a bag of groceries in her arms.

"Didn't you hear me calling you?" she asked in an annoyed voice. "I've been trying to catch up with you for half a block."

"I'm sorry, Mrs. French. I wasn't paying any attention."

"I should say you weren't." She was out of breath from hurrying.

Shera made a move as if to go on in.

"Just a minute," the landlady said. "I have something I need to talk to you about."

"What is it?" Shera said impatiently.

"I thought I heard some hammering up there in your place yesterday, and you know that there aren't to be any nail holes in my walls or you won't get your deposit back."

Shera started moving up the stairs, and Mrs. French followed. "I promise, Mrs. French, I haven't been doing any hammering. I don't even have a hammer."

"Well, that boyfriend of yours, he might. Is he living here now?"

Shera blushed and stammered. "T-T-Tony? He, uh, lives with his mother." Nosy old woman.

The landlady looked skeptical. "Well, you just make sure he knows my rules." They were at the door. "And that yelling is going to have to stop. You're disturbing everyone in the building."

Shera nodded and hurried up the stairs. Once inside her apartment she locked the door behind her, then turned on a table lamp. It wasn't dark yet outside, but the multistoried apartment buildings brought twilight early. She watched the movements of people below from the window, her vantage point on the world, then walked distractedly to the refrigerator and opened it. There wasn't much in it, so she shut it and wandered back to the window.

If only Tony had trusted her, she wouldn't have gone to the police. If he had only asked her to help him.

What would happen to Tony if they connected him to the car? Maybe it wasn't her car anyway—just a lookalike. There were lots of cars just like hers around; she saw them all the time. She had a gut-level feeling it was her car, though.

What if they don't connect Tony to it, but they find out it was my car for sure? she thought. Does that make me responsible? Could they charge me with something?

There were so many unanswered questions she was getting a headache. She found some aspirin and took them to the tiny bathroom where she kept a pearlized, pink plastic tumbler beside the lavatory. After she swallowed the tablets, she returned to the bedroom and lay down on the ribcord bedspread without undressing, fumbling to unfasten the snap on her jeans because the waist cut into her middle. She pulled her eyebrows together, unable to banish all her questions.

I'll call that insurance woman back tomorrow, she thought. She was smart, and I can talk to her.

She realized she hadn't gotten the information from the police that the insurance company had wanted, but it didn't matter now anyway. Everything had changed. She wouldn't be telling that woman who she was.

The throbbing of her headache began to subside, and she curled her knees up toward her chest and drifted off to sleep.

Tony came in much later, smelling of stale cigarettes and beer. The sound of the key in the lock had wakened Shera from a fitful sleep, but it took her a moment to recall what she was doing in bed with her clothes on. Then it came back to her.

She lay very still as Tony, not undressing, pulled the bedspread and sheet back and got into bed beside her. She didn't want him to know she was awake, didn't want to talk about the car tonight. Tomorrow, while he still slept, she would call the insurance woman.

To Shera, their secrets were like a barrier erected down the center of the bed. And the bedspread on which she lay, and which covered him, well, that was the way it was in life. She was an outsider, unprotected. No one had ever cared enough for her. Not her mother nor her father; not Tony. He had made her feel good about herself for a while, but now she knew it was ending. And this thing today—not telling her the truth—that proved it.

The night shadows of the room magnified her loneliness, and she began to cry silently into the pillow. She had no one.

3

Lora had missed Brad that day at break, but about quitting time he'd passed through the department, scattering his charm like flu germs. He was wearing a well-fitting lightweight gray suit, a white shirt, and a quiet gray and burgundy tie—dressed for success. As if he had felt her eyes upon him, he glanced over and caught her staring. If being caught wasn't bad enough, he'd winked—and she had blushed.

Now, as she prepared her evening meal—a salad—she found herself thinking about that wink. Had he meant anything by it? He had never winked at her before. She chided herself for trying to read something into it.

I must really be getting desperate. I may have to call

Jack, she thought, poking fun at herself. She remembered the first time she had met Jack.

"Hey, there, anyone home?"

Lora heard the voice and came hurrying down the hallway on the first evening she had been in the house. It was late summer, and she hadn't heard the sound of her own voice all day, let alone someone else's. A man stood at the front screen, his forearm resting against the door at an angle over his head. She was glad the hook was latched, although it wouldn't have been much protection against this strapping man of, say, forty-five, hair thinning on top but bushy brown on the sides. His tanned skin looked as if it came right off the golf course, but his middle looked as if it came from a corner beer joint. Bristly hair protruded from the neck of his golf shirt.

"Hi, I'm Jack Turner," he said, taking stock of her. "I live right over there." He turned the upper half of his torso to point with one arm while continuing to lean on the other against the door. Very relaxed.

She smiled. "I'm Lora Montgomery. Glad to meet you."

"Just thought I'd drop over and introduce myself, make you feel welcome, see if there was anything I could do for you folks."

She let the allusion to another person slide by uncorrected. "That's nice of you. Come on in." She unlatched the door. "You're the first neighbor I've met. And maybe there is something you can do for me." She'd had a brainstorm, but quickly squelched it. "Oh, I hate to impose—"

"No, really," he assured her, "I came to help if I can."

"Do you know how to hook up a washer? Maybe you could tell me— "

"I can take care of it." He followed her into the laundry alcove behind the kitchen.

"Your old man doesn't do this sort of thing?"

"I'm not married."

"Pretty thing like you? C'mon, what's the world coming to?"

She smiled at the easygoing flattery. "I have been. I'm divorced." Still hard to say it.

He got a serious look on his face. "He must have been a fool."

It made her uncomfortable, and she blushed. She was too newly divorced to recognize his talk for what it was.

He was busy attaching the hoses to the faucets. "Do you have some pliers?"

She got them for him. He tightened the connections, then shoved the washer back as far as it would go. Quite easily, too, considering what a job it would have been for her.

"All done," he said.

"Well, thanks. I really appreciate it. I would have probably had to pay a serviceman a small fortune. May I pay—"

He shook his head emphatically.

"I do happen to have some beer. Would you like one?"

"Now you're talking my language, lady."

She took two beers out of the refrigerator and popped the tabs. She had moved them from the apartment where they had been in the refrigerator for several months, since Martin, her ex-husband, had helped her move from the house they had shared.

She and Jack sat down at the breakfast bar. He took a long swig of his beer. "You may need a man around here sometime, to help with something, so you know who you can call now. I'm close."

She nodded.

"And handy," he added. He looked at her in an intimate sort of way which made her uncomfortable.

She looked down at the beer and traced her finger through the sweat on the can. "Are you married?"

"Separated. And I want to tell you, after over twenty years of marriage, it gets kind of lonely over there."

"I guess it would. Have you ever thought about divorce?"

"Forget it." He snorted. "She'd bleed me dry. I'm already living like a squatter compared to her." He waved his arm toward his house. "Would you believe I have a ten-room house in University Park? This was just one of my investments."

"What do you do for a living, Mr. Turner?"

"Jack," he said. "Hell, I just installed your washer, the least you can do is call me Jack. Right?"

She nodded slightly. "Jack."

He licked some foam off his lips. "I'm an attorney."

Flustered at finding out he was a professional, Lora said, "Oh, my, I'm sorry I imposed on you."

He waved off her apology. "I told you I'm handy." His accompanying smile was suggestive.

Lora stood up, feeling a little giddy from the beer, and said, "Well, I guess I'd better get busy with this . . ." She gestured around at the boxes cluttering the floor, ". . . or I'll be unpacking till Christmas. Thanks again for the help." Realizing he was being dismissed, Jack stood up and went into the living room. Lora followed.

His last statement as he went through the door left her uneasy. "Now remember to call me if you need anything." The emphasis seemed to be on the *anything*.

Sometimes when she was alone she would look across

the street at his lights and come ever so close to calling him up. What would it matter? she would think. He was a warm body, wasn't he? It was usually about the middle of the month, when all her nerve endings seemed alive with sexual tension wanting release. It was nature's little prod toward continuity, she guessed, coming mid-month, as it did. Except with her the prod hadn't worked. She had never gotten pregnant, though she and Martin had tried.

She'd had a series of tests that didn't show anything wrong with her, but Martin had refused to have any. So without medical verification to the contrary, she would go on assuming she was fertile. Not that it was going to make any difference if she waited much longer. She felt a small stab of pain at the thought of not having any children. If she only had some now, she thought, she surely wouldn't feel so . . . so . . . what? Alone, she guessed. With a child, she would have a focus.

When she and Martin had divorced, she'd had her doctor insert an IUD, just in case she met Mr. Right. But so far that had been an exercise in futility; nearly a year now and no Mr. Right had turned up, not even a Mr. Possibly. And no Jack.

She tore iceberg lettuce leaves apart tenderly, arranging them carefully in an individual-sized wooden salad bowl. Then she sliced some radishes and a carrot. Neatly, she cut some ham and cheese slices into julienne strips and laid them across the lettuce, then topped the whole arrangement with several rings of sliced bell pepper. Very attractive. She wrapped the leftover vegetables in plastic and stuck them in the refrigerator for another night's salad, removing the blue-cheese dressing at the same time. She added some to the salad and tossed it slightly, watching her careful creation be destroyed.

A wink, she thought, as she carried her salad to the table, seemed so automatic to some people, as automatic as the repeated use of a trite phrase in conversation. Some people's winks seemed filled with humor, but not Brad's. His carried a sexual innuendo, as most of his behavior did. It bordered on sexual harassment, except he was so attractive you forgave it. He seemed exploitive, but now she was . . . wanting to be exploited? Perhaps so. Just being singled out by him, even with a wink, was exciting. She began to fantasize about his six-foot-tall, wide-shouldered frame—not undressed though, just holding her.

Lora snapped back to reality, eating a salad, alone, with poor prospects. More fantasizing about Brad and she would be a basket case by bedtime.

She slowly ate her salad. She was trying to do what the self-help books suggested by taking care of herself, trying to maintain, and perhaps even develop, self-esteem. What she really wanted to eat was a candy bar and Coke. But that would not be taking care of herself. So she went through the motions of caring. Why did having a man to prepare meals for, to share them with, make food preparation and consumption a more valued activity? Was it society, Martin, or she who had brought her to this self-devaluation? If she had cared enough about him to provide nutritional meals, why did she resent doing it for herself?

She sat alone at her small Formica table, eating the nutritious salad and hating it.

When she finished, she took her salad bowl to the kitchen, squirted liquid detergent into it, swished it around with her hand, then rinsed and dried it. She shook some instant tea into a glass, not wanting to get out a spoon, dropped in several ice cubes, then ran tap water vigorously into it to mix it up. She placed the half-empty ice tray back in the freezer. She would watch a *M.A.S.H.* rerun, then maybe go somewhere.

This particular episode had been on two, maybe three times. It was the one in which Colonel Blake's plane crashes. She hadn't seen it during prime time, not having watched until the reruns started. She sipped her iced tea, shoeless feet on the coffee table, engrossed with these characters she now knew so well. She almost knew some of the lines by heart. It was comforting, companionable. Television was a great tranquilizer. She nursed her iced tea as if it were a mixed drink.

When the show was over, she slipped on her shoes, located her purse and stepped outside, locking the door behind her.

Lora felt the loneliness of twilight acutely as she glanced down the street, its flaws softened now by dusk. Lights were beginning to come on in the houses, bathing the family lives inside in rich yellow warmth. Or that's how the situation looked from the outside, but she knew it was an illusion. Some of those lives were as lonely as hers.

Even Jack's house looked inviting. There was a strange car parked outside. She wondered if he had inveigled someone to come over to help him cope. She shrugged, making no judgment. Everyone has his own way. Then she thought ruefully what a distance her attitudes had traveled in a year. She had been pretty strait-laced about anyone involved in extramarital affairs. Judgmental. Well, now she was on the other side of the fence, and things just weren't quite so clear anymore. Right, wrong—they were muddled. When the values you grew up believing stop working, when they don't seem to reflect the real world, maybe you have to change, she reflected, to march in step with everyone else.

Jack had, perhaps, found a way to stave off loneliness. She would ease her car out of the driveway and down the street toward the nearest shopping center, knowing that once she reached its bright lights she could momentarily stave off her brand of loneliness. She would assuage it with a purchase, a concrete acquisition, something to hang onto. She would buy a momentary bit of happiness.

4

The call came in first thing the next morning. Lora could pinpoint it later because she was still trying to get her headset adjusted comfortably without messing up her hair.

She was sleepy; coffee hadn't helped yet. When she had returned home the evening before, she hadn't even unpacked her new purchase, a blouse. She just sat down in front of the TV again, mesmerized by the comforting movement and noise. Martin, her ex, had called just to see how things were going, and she'd been tempted to ask him over for the night—she thought that was why he waited so late to call—but overcame the temptation.

After their brief conversation, she had gone back to the television until one. And now she was paying for it. She yawned, trying to suppress it, and patted her hair into place.

Just then her extension buzzed.

"Claims. Lora speaking," she said automatically.

The voice was odd, kind of breathy and very close to the telephone receiver, but Lora didn't particularly take note at the time because she had heard them all, it seemed. "I—I wonder if you c-can give me some information?"

"Maybe," Lora said. "What is it you need to know?" She noticed a rough place on her fingernail and pulled an emery board from the tray at the front of her desk drawer.

"Are you still there?" Lora asked after the person didn't respond.

"Yes."

"What is it I can help you with?" She ran the emery board along her nail in one direction, the heel of her hand resting on her open drawer, systematically obliterating the roughness.

"If—If my car was involved in a . . ." The woman paused for a deep audible breath. Lora expected her to say "accident" and was surprised when the caller said instead, "hit-and-run." She could understand now why the person was reluctant to speak. Lora had come to attention at the words, the emery board frozen in passage, but the caller didn't have a chance to say any more. Her sentence was ripped open by a scream, then a crash as the phone dropped. The sound reverberated in Lora's ear, and she momentarily pulled the earpiece away. Then, curious, she listened again.

A man's voice was exploding in a steady stream of obscenities. "You slitch, you goddamn filthy slitch. I should have known not to trust you, you fucking whore." He continued to spew out the degrading words.

"No, no! You don't understand," Lora heard the woman plead. "I didn't—stop, please, please—" Her voice became muffled, then silent. The other voice didn't. Its rage shot across the distance between the phones as brutally as if the man were actually there. Except it was all auditory.

The incongruity was that Lora's eyes were still focused on a steel and fluorescent world—serene, cold, and orderly.

The man's anger became more subdued. But what about the woman? Lora wondered. What had happened to her? The line itself had become silent. "Hello? Hello?" Lora said into the phone. "Are you there?"

A voice came to her ears. The man. "Who is this?" shot into the phone. His voice was filled with cold fury. Then, more insistently, he said, "Who the hell is this?"

Lora, scarcely breathing, quickly disconnected. She was holding the emery board poised for another stroke.

What could she do? The woman was in obvious trouble, but was it just a domestic problem? She didn't know the woman's name or where she was calling from, except somewhere in the state of New York.

Lora rubbed the frown that had formed between her eyebrows and pulled her headset off. There didn't seem to be anything to do.

"Hey, there, beautiful, what's the matter? Got a headache?" It was Brad. She had been watching him every chance she got for days, and here she'd missed him when he walked right to her desk. His voice snapped her back to reality.

"What? Oh, uh, no," she said, hurriedly reconstructing what he'd just said.

He shrugged. "You were rubbing your forehead."

"I just had a strange call."

"Don't worry about it. You'll get wrinkles. Anyhow, don't you get weirdos all the time? What was so special this time?"

She hesitated, wanting to describe it accurately, but Brad filled the momentary void, saying, "Haven't seen you in the lounge for a day or so."

She attempted to shift mental gears by tipping her head to one side and saying in a voice she at least hoped sounded seductive, "My hard luck, huh?" She began to play with a lock of her hair.

Brad responded by grinning at her, his lids lowered. "How about having dinner with me this evening and I'll show you how your luck can change."

She tried to keep her voice even, though she was excited by this coup; her pulse had quickened. "Sure, that would be nice, if you have time in your busy schedule for me."

"I'll make time for you," he responded, with the emphasis on the *you*. "I'll just come by here on my way out."

Her extension buzzed. She nodded and smiled as she readjusted her headset. Brad winked and turned to go.

The old saws seemed still to hold grains of truth: absence makes the heart grow fonder. A few days of not seeing her had piqued Brad's interest. She shuddered slightly at the thought that she was once again involved in all the games of dating.

5

Tony slammed down the receiver in a fury, his teeth clenched and his hand quivering. He started to turn away, then noticed the insurance card Shera had dropped as she'd fallen. He picked it up and scanned it, his eyes becoming dark. So that's what she was doing, the little slitch. Goddamn her, he thought, causing me even more problems than I already have.

She was still lying on the floor. He looked at her a moment, expecting her to come to, expecting her to move lethargically, as if waking from a nap. What had she told that person on the phone? Had she talked to the police? No, he simply couldn't believe she would go behind his back and call them when he'd told her not to. But she sure as hell had called someone. And she sure as hell had asked about a hit-and-run. He looked at the card in his hand again. It must have been the insurance company, but what in the crap was she thinking of, anyway? He'd have to find out, one way or another.

He went over to where the young woman lay on the floor and prodded her with his toe. "Damn it, Shera, get up."

He bent down, aware that his slacks were wet where they stretched across his thighs. He shook his head in disgust at the sensation. It had happened when he knocked her down—he had soared then, his mind exploding, his body seeming to redefine itself, making contact with something infinitely pleasurable.

But now the feeling was gone; he was anesthetized. He gave Shera an abrupt shake, then straightened back up and stared at the body, his eyes crinkling into slits.

"Oh, Jesus," he muttered aloud, running both hands back through his thick dark hair. The muscle at one corner of his mouth began to twitch. He knelt down once again and felt her neck for a pulse. There was none.

"Oh, Jesus," he repeated. He stared at her blank face and felt the prickly sweat gather at his hairline.

He got up, jammed the insurance card into his pocket

and walked toward the bathroom. He needed time, time to think about what to do, but first he had to clean himself up. He hated to be dirty.

He went into the bedroom and looked in the closet for a pair of clean jeans or slacks, but didn't find any. He even looked under the bed, in case Shera had shoved some under there. She hadn't been much of a housekeeper when he'd first started coming there, but now she kept things clean, because he liked the apartment that way. Every once in a while, though, he would find reminders of her formerly slovenly ways—underwear pushed under the bed in haste when she heard him coming, that sort of thing.

He went into the tiny bathroom and cleaned himself up. Reluctantly, he put his same jeans back on. He held the hair dryer to the wet spot, and impatient about how long it took the denim to show any sign of drying, he held the nozzle closer. The smell of scorching fabric began to fill the little room. Finally, he slammed the dryer down on the back of the toilet, knocking a bottle of hand lotion to the floor. He didn't bother to pick it up. Coming out of the bathroom cursing, he snatched a pack of cigarettes from the floor beside the couch, where he'd dropped them the day before. He nervously pulled one out, tapped it against his wrist even though it was filtered, and fumbled for the disposable lighter in his pocket. He inhaled deeply with the first drag.

God, what a day, he thought. He fell back onto the couch, his legs stretched out before him. The feel of the damp fabric made him wonder why beating on someone got him off.

When he first met Shera, his sex play had been playfully rough. It made it better for him, and he could tell she had liked it. But his appetite for the roughness grew, and lately he needed to be abusive just to feel sexually satisfied. Was it only with Shera? She was so passive. What would it be like with a different kind of woman, one who had a mind of her own? He often fantasized, but never acted on his daydreams. He had always gone out with women who could be molded into any shape he chose; he always picked the same type, and he guessed he wasn't going to change now. All his girlfriends seemed to be cast in the mold of his mother: whiny, ineffectual.

He knew he was partially responsible for the way Shera had become. When he met her, she'd seemed infinitely malleable, just because of the way she obviously felt about him. So he was sure he could have shaped her to be assertive, if he'd wanted to, but instead he promoted her dependence and insecurity. He liked to keep her slightly off-balance. That's why he left most of his things at his mother's and went to the trouble to go there mornings to dress for work. That way he didn't give up his autonomy; neither of the women in his life, Shera or his mother, became too sure of him. He didn't consider this complication he had manufactured to be fragmenting; on the contrary, it felt more as if it maintained his integrity. He didn't want any woman to get the idea she owned him.

But, damn, he had felt sure of *Shera,* hadn't expected her to call anyone about the car, not after he'd told her not to. She had adored him, he knew that. Nevertheless his "We're not going to call the police" must have fallen on deaf ears the day before.

He angrily stubbed out his half-smoked cigarette, stood up and strode across the room. His gaze took in the small living room, with its bland, beige walls sadly in need of paint, its requisite rose-beige nylon pile couch and matching armchair, its blond Formica-topped coffee and end tables and bargain store ceramic lamp. His eyes swept to the small kitchenette. It had a round wooden table at one end, painted white, a six-foot metal sink unit along the middle wall beyond his view, facing the gas range and an old oversized Kelvinator refrigerator. Everything looked normal, but there was Shera's body in the middle of the floor, changing his life.

She could have been asleep—she looked so relaxed in her blue jeans, one knee bent up comfortably, her lank ponytail flung out on the floor in an inverted question mark. He walked over to her. She looked so much as if she were just sleeping that he thought perhaps she'd started breathing while he was in the bathroom. It would sure save him a lot of trouble. But no. He studied her body for a moment, but it remained still.

He would give anything to do a replay of the last twenty-four hours. But she was dead, and the immediate problem needed to be solved—what to do with the body. He couldn't just call the undertaker. He couldn't just pick it up and carry it out of the building—though for all the neighbors in this building cared, he probably could. But he wouldn't try. You never knew. This would be the time someone who didn't give a shit for a person alive turned into a best friend when she turned up dead.

He sat there trying to think of someone who owed him one, someone whose aid he could enlist. Someone from the underbelly of New York who could be counted on not to care one way or the other about a life or a death. He couldn't think of anyone he could trust, no friend who would do or die for him. His mother would, of course, but she wouldn't be any help; she would get hysterical. Oddly enough, he realized, the only person he could have counted on in this kind of a pinch was there, dead, before him.

The muscle at the corner of his mouth had begun to twitch again. He needed a beer to help him relax. He drew his fingers through his hair in frustration and, out of habit, went to the refrigerator and opened the door.

Shit, he thought, his anger mounting instantaneously, she didn't even get me any more beer, like I told her to. He immediately felt silly about his reaction, remembering the body on the floor. The beer was what had made him angry yesterday afternoon, when he stormed out. He hadn't come back till late, groggy from drink, falling into bed fully clothed. If there had been beer yesterday, he probably wouldn't have left, probably would have told her why her car wasn't by the curb where she'd left it when she went to work, instead of feeding her that line about it being stolen. And probably he would have told her about the hit-and-run, engaging her sympathy. And probably none of this would have happened. Probably. Probably. But that was hindsight, which didn't do a helluva lot of good now.

The refrigerator was almost bare. There was a jar of pickle juice with one last whole kosher dill floating in it like a bloated fish, some crumpled butcher paper half concealing a dried-out slice of bologna, a bottle of taco sauce, a jar of salad dressing, three eggs in the door, and an open stick of margarine smashed at one end, where Shera had greased a pan with it. That was all. No beer.

The body fit snugly into the refrigerator, once he removed the shelves and put all the stuff in the trash. He stashed the shelves between the refrigerator and the sink unit. The idea was gross to him, putting a body in a refrigerator, the same refrigerator where you put your food, but it solved the immediate problem, which had to be his main concern right now, so he just divorced himself from thinking about it. More than anything, he needed time to assess his situation. Maybe something would happen to make it clear what he should do, maybe something would occur to him.

The body could be in there for quite a while, he imagined, without starting to smell bad. The neighbors, as long as they were left alone, wouldn't notice a thing wrong. Shera hadn't known any of them, so they wouldn't miss her. And the rent was paid up for a couple more weeks, so the bitch of a landlady wouldn't be a problem.

How had Shera found out about the hit-and-run? He would probably never know. But the fact was that he walked in while she was talking about the hit-and-run on the phone. And Shera was dead.

He shook his head, unable to understand it. He ran his fingers along the top of the refrigerator, absent-mindedly checking his fingertips for dust. He screwed up his face, wondering why Shera had called the insurance company. It didn't make sense. Maybe, he thought, she had heard about the hit-and-run on the radio. Surely she was just surmising that it might be her car. He pushed from his mind the idea that she might have reported her missing car to the police, not when he had ordered her not to.

She had really thrown him for a loop. Where had that spark of initiative come from? Well, he hadn't told her *not* to call the insurance company, so she hadn't really disobeyed him about that, but what a dumb thing anyway. What would they know about it? Tony smiled.

He felt a little better, thinking that. But then he remembered that person on the other end of that line; there had been someone there, listening. His smile faded. He shook his head in consternation, unable to sort it all out. Maybe a beer would help. Besides, he had to get out of here.

6

"You aren't going to believe what happened to me," Lora told her friend Sue Evans as they walked to the lounge for coffee.

"Want me to guess? I saw Brad lolling around by your desk this morning."

"He asked me to go to dinner."

"And you're going to tell me that you accepted."

Lora nodded, a sheepish smile on her face.

"Crazy girl. You're too good for him."

"You just don't understand."

"Of course I do. There are not that many eligible men floating around. I've heard that before."

"Desirable ones."

They had reached the lounge, and Sue put money into the coffee machine. "That term, 'desirable,' is where we disagree about Brad," Sue remarked.

"Well, maybe when I was your age I could have been more choosy, but do your realize this will be the first real date I've had since Martin and I divorced?"

"You've just been particular, that's all. But Brad is a strange one to suddenly lower your standards for."

Lora had gotten a cup of coffee, too, and now they wound their way to a table by the window.

"I guess I'm just getting desperate."

Another claims representative from their department overheard her remark. She draped herself into a chair at their table with a "Mind if I join you? Now what are you getting desperate about, Lora?"

"Dating and all its ramifications, L.J."

"Why be desperate?" she asked around the straw in her Dr Pepper. "Just do whatever comes naturally."

Sue was listening with a frown. "Now don't be giving Lora any of your free advice, and I mean 'free' very literally," she added in grave tones.

L.J. made a face. She was in her mid-twenties, blond, blue-eyed, willowy, and tan year-round. She looked like she belonged in California, which she represented for the company, but she was from Wichita, Kansas. She had migrated right down I-35 two years earlier, hoping to find more excitement in Dallas.

"Okay, you two," Lora said with a laugh. "I can take care of myself." It was odd, Lora thought, to hear these two disagreeing on life-styles. Both were light-years away from her. Sue had been living with a man, Kevin, for two years now, and the California rep had a steady stream of lovers, or so the gossip said. "I would probably do well to take some advice from L.J. I don't seem to have any luck meeting men."

"Well," L.J. said lazily, "you can't sit home and do it. They don't come through the living room."

Lora smiled. "I've noticed that. I went to a bar once—"

Sue looked startled. "You did?"

Lora nodded. "Right when I first got divorced. I thought I'd show Martin. Well, anyway, I went in and ordered. Then I sat there. When I finished my drink, I left. No one tried to pick me up; no one even talked to me. It was awful. There I was, putting myself out in the marketplace—boldly, for me—and I was rejected."

"Yeah, and you probably stared at the ice cubes in your drink all the time you were there," L.J. said. "was it a singles bar?"

"I don't know. But I should have gone with someone; I wouldn't have felt like such a wallflower."

"I don't ever go with someone; another person would just get in the way. But you have to look around, pick someone you're interested in and let them know it. Most guys aren't going to hit on you if you look like you're going to reject them. And I would definitely go to a singles bar. Who wants to have to sift through the chaff at a regular bar?"

"I think the whole notion of 'selling' yourself at a bar is degrading," Sue said. "And dangerous. I think you're a fool, L.J., and—"

"Listen, Susie," L.J. said patronizingly, "I can take care of myself without any—"

Lora could see that the conversation was going downhill, so she changed the subject. "Hey, I got a really strange call this morning."

"What was it, obscene?" Sue asked. "I got one of those once at home. Somebody asked if I would participate in a survey he was doing. Naturally," she said broadly, "I like to get my two cents in whenever I can, so I agreed. Well, it turned out his survey was about sex. He was some kind of pervert. After I hung up, I rushed around the house closing all the drapes. It made me really nervous, because he had invaded my own personal space." She said the last with her teeth clenched firmly together.

"The one I got wasn't like that. I answered, figuring it would be routine, because the person said she—let's see now,'' Lora said thoughtfully, ''how was it . . . she wondered if I could give her some information. That's how she started out. I thought she was going to ask about her car being involved in an accident, but instead she said 'hit-and-run.' Just then someone hit her or something; she dropped the phone and all I could hear were a lot of obscenities—a man's voice—and this woman pleading with him. He called her . . . a slitch.''

The California rep screwed her nose up. ''That's a new one.'' Her comment made it obvious that she was listening, but her eyes were constantly scanning the room.

Lora nodded. ''He was so brutal sounding, the way he was yelling.''

''Pardon me, guys, gotta go talk to someone,'' L.J. said, picking up her soft drink. The two of them watched as she made her way to a table where a young man sat alone. Sue mumbled something unkind and shook her head.

''Sue, I do believe you're more puritanical than I am,'' Lora commented.

''I just can't believe how obvious she is. Go on and tell me about the call,'' Sue said. ''What finally happened?''

Lora shrugged. ''I didn't hear the woman again, but the man came on and asked who I was.''

''You didn't tell him, did you?''

Lora shook her head. ''I disconnected.''

''Did you call the police?''

''I really don't have anything to tell them. I don't know her name, or even where she was, other than the state of New York.''

''Look at the odds, though. Don't most of your calls come from New York City?''

''Yes.''

"Well, then you could call the police in each of the boroughs—in fact, probably just one could tell you if there had been a hit-and-run anywhere in the state—the way they communicate these days."

"You're probably right. Sue, you're a regular Nancy Drew type."

"Gee, thanks, I read every one of those—right from *The Secret in the Old Clock.* Unfortunately, I think I'm more like Nancy's friend George."

Lora laughed. "Hardly." They talked a moment about the innocence of a time when a heroine could have a female friend named George with no social implications. "I think you're right, though, that I should call the police. I could just tell them she mentioned a hit-and-run," she mused, toying with a piece of her hair with one hand, "and if her car was involved in one and her question wasn't just hypothetical, then maybe they'd know about it. I mean, there couldn't be too many hit-and-runs in a day, could there?"

"Maybe in New York. But they could check it out, and if she's a suspect, they could see what happened to her, what you heard. My, this is really exciting, isn't it?" Sue was almost squirming in her seat.

"But why would she call me if she were a suspect in a hit-and-run? She'd know all she wanted to know, wouldn't she? I mean, she'd know if she did it. And if she didn't, well . . ." She shrugged.

"What would I do if I were involved in a hit-and-run?" Sue pondered.

"Oh, wait. That's it. She wasn't involved. She said her car was involved."

Sue nodded in understanding. "Ah, I see. She wasn't in it at the time. So maybe her husband was. And he came in and heard her talking on the phone about it."

"That would make him angry, all right."

"Maybe he confided in her, and since she couldn't call the police, she thought of us. You know we do all that advertising, saying what pals we are in times of trouble," Sue said.

"It must be working."

"The trouble with that explanation is why would she care about her car? I mean at a time like this." Sue frowned. "If she tried to make a claim or anything, the car would be implicated, leading right back to the husband."

"Maybe she wasn't thinking too straight," Lora suggested.

"No doubt."

"Still, I could unload it on the police, and I think I would feel better about it. They're not too crazy about getting involved in domestic problems, though."

"Yeah, but this involves a hit-and-run."

"Well, I'll call them and see what they say."

Sue glanced at her watch. "Hey, we'd better get back."

They tossed their empty cups in the trash container and returned to their department. "See you later, Lora," Sue said. "And watch it tonight."

Putting the call through to the NYPD didn't take long because Lora had the number handy, but then they began to transfer her call and she got put on hold twice, until she finally got routed to Bill Graham's desk. There, she was put on hold again, till they found him. She was about to give up in exasperation when he came on the line.

"Lieutenant Graham."

"You're not going to put me on hold, are you?" she asked.

"I hadn't planned on it. What can I do for you?"

"My name is Lora Montgomery and I'm an insurance

claims representative,'' she began for the third time. ''I work out of Dallas, but I cover claims called in from New York.''

''I thought I detected a Texas accent. I was down there when I was in the service. El Paso—quite a way from Dallas.''

''Yes, it is. I've never been there.''

''Sorry I interrupted. You were saying . . . ?''

''Well, this morning I got a strange call which I think I maybe should report.'' She went on to tell him about it.

''The reason you were turned over to me,'' he told her after she had finished her recital, ''is because I'm handling a hit-and-run case which coincides with the approximate time frame you're talking about.''

''I realize what I've told you can't be of much help,'' Lora said. ''I don't even have a name or anything.''

''That's too bad, because we really need a lead right now on this hit-and-run. We haven't found the vehicle, and we're pretty much at a standstill. Let me get your number there, so I can reach you if I need to call you back.''

She gave him the number, feeling very much like a Girl Scout who has just done a good deed, or perhaps a busybody. Not that Bill Graham didn't act interested. His thanks seemed very sincere.

''Well, that's behind me,'' she murmured to herself as she prepared to take an incoming call.

7

Tony's mother was watching her soap opera when he came in, but she broke her attention to jump up, go over and try to give him a hug. Tony pulled away. It hurt her feelings, his coolness, because he was all she had now that her husband was dead.

She dropped her hands and wiped them unconsciously on the terry-cloth apron that covered the ample middle of her blue and lavender flowered-print dress. Some wiry gray hairs were escaping from the bun that sat on top of her head like a tiara, giving her a slightly disheveled but thoroughly domestic look.

"Would you like me to make you some lunch? I bet you haven't eaten."

"Don't bother. I'm okay."

"It's no bother," she said, with only the slightest glance at her soap opera, still in progress.

"Okay, Mama, whatever you want," he said.

Tony went to his room to shower while she rummaged through the refrigerator, trying to decide what to prepare for him. Her cat, Miss Kitty, came up beside her and rubbed against her ankle and meowed, just as she did every time Anna Longoria opened the refrigerator.

"Tony's home, Miss Kitty. Aren't we lucky? I'm going to fix him a bite to eat." Nodding, she pulled out a block of cheese. "He'll like this."

8

Tony was relieved to be in his own room, away from her, away from the inevitable questions. And then the nagging followed. He resented it like hell.

He remembered a snowy evening when he and Mama and Daddy were going to walk to Aunt Mary's, Mama's sister's, for Friday night supper. They were about ready to go when Tony announced that he didn't want to wear the new galoshes his mama had bought for him.

"You have to wear them, Sonny. You'll catch cold."

"No," the little boy said belligerently. "I don't want to wear them."

"Yes, you have to," she insisted.

His father interceded. "Let him go, Anna. He doesn't need galoshes. Especially those red girl galoshes."

"They're not girls' galoshes," his mother protested. "And I got them for almost nothing on sale," she said defensively.

"I don't want to wear girl galoshes," Tony piped in.

"They're not girls'," his mother said. "And you'll

catch a cold if you don't wear them.'' Her voice had become whiny.

''Anna, I said he didn't have to wear them.'' His father shoved her up against the wall. ''Goddamn it,'' he shouted, ''when I say something, I want you to pay attention. How is this boy ever going to learn any respect?''

''I'm sorry.''

''You'll *be* sorry.'' He twisted her arm.

''Joe, you're hurting me.'' His mother began to cry.

''Stop that goddamn sniveling!'' his father shouted.

Tony directed his interest elsewhere. The galoshes. He began to pull them on and struggle with the clasps. He blocked out the sounds of his father slapping his mother around as she tried to stop her crying. He just focused on the boots that had caused all the trouble. The next thing he knew, his father's attention was focused on him. Tony's eyes widened in fear. Was he to be next? He had put the boots on, disobeying Daddy. Hurriedly, his little fingers grasped at the clasps, trying to undo them, but they just wouldn't work.

But Daddy didn't beat him. He just growled at him, ''Get those goddamn sissy boots off. No boy of mine is gonna wear sissy things.''

Shortly afterward they went to Aunt Mary's, just as if nothing had happened. Everything appeared normal, except Tony felt, way back in his head somewhere, as if he'd done something bad, though he wasn't sure what. He got his feet wet that night, going to Aunt Mary's, and a few days later he came down with a cold.

It was the first time he remembered his father hitting his mother. After that it wasn't unusual. It happened every Friday night after his father came home from the bar where he stopped after work on Fridays to celebrate the end of the week. The beatings were almost a family tradition.

Purple, yellow, and green bruises on his mother's sausagelike arms. New ones before the old ones faded. On her once pretty skin.

One morning when he was about thirteen, eating a bowl of Wheaties at the Formica breakfast table, something in him clicked. It was a Saturday, and his father had come in drunk the night before and had flown into a rage about something so trivial he couldn't remember what it was. Tony's mother came slogging down the hall to the kitchen in a blue chenille bathrobe. She had a black eye this time. She stood in front of the stove, her pride as shriveled as the bacon she was frying—preparing a fine breakfast for a man who had beaten her the night before.

Maybe Tony could say something to help. "Mama," he started, reaching out, tipping over his milk glass.

Mama turned. "Now see what you've done. You clumsy. Get a towel and clean that up. When will you learn to be careful? You're as bad as your father."

Who was she to be talking to him like that? Fat slitch. He started to call her that out loud, but held it back. She was nothing. He might have wept, but instead he was repulsed by her. Women like her deserved beating because they were so stupid. His father and Uncle Ray were right. . . .

He remembered sitting out on the long porch one hot summer night when everyone else along the street was trying to cool off and he was just enjoying the things of childhood—trapping bugs, drawing pictures in the dirt below the steps. His father and Uncle Ray were relaxing on the porch while Mama did the dishes inside. Lights were winking on in houses along the street. Tony was peeling tiny patches of paint off of the front porch for entertainment and listening to the drone of the men's voices.

"Women are bitches, Joe," Ray said. "All of 'em."

Joe snorted, taking a cigarette Ray offered him, tapping it on the back of his hand before he stuck it in his mouth. "Now, Ray, just because you and Ruby have split the sheet doesn't mean they're all bad. Throw me your matches." He lit up, then leaned back on two legs of his chair.

"Sluts, Joe. Look at those bitches down there trying to sell it. Goddamn, look at 'em. Who'd want it?" He gestured down the street toward the neighborhood drugstore, where two women leaned against a phone booth. "They all just take advantage of us poor men." He rubbed his crotch.

Tony focused his attention momentarily on the drugstore. Was it for sale? He hoped not because he liked to go there to buy things. They had all the comic books down where he could look through them.

"Is the drugstore for sale?" he asked, his little face squeezed into a frown.

Uncle Ray laughed and Joe grinned.

"Is it, Daddy?"

"Nah," his father answered. The end of his cigarette glowed in the deepening gloom of the porch. The two men sat quietly a moment.

Tony shoved some sand into a doodlebug pit and waited for the hidden insect to toss it back out, but it was getting too dark to see if there was any activity in the tiny pitfall of the insect. "Daddy," he asked his father while they were sitting quietly, "what's a slitch?"

"A what?" his father asked.

Ray caught on first and guffawed. "A slitch, you bastard. Don't you know what a slitch is? Your boy's smarter than you."

Joe looked perplexed for a minute.

Ray went on. "It's a cross between a slut and a bitch. Anthony may have made up a riddle here. Smart kid." He reached over and tousled Tony's hair with his hand. Tony frowned.

"You got a slut," Joe said, catching on, "and I got a bitch." He laughed around the cigarette which drooped from his mouth.

"Past tense, Joe. I had a slut." He leaned confidentially toward Tony. "A slitch, Anthony. But Uncle Ray is no dope."

"What's a slitch, Uncle Ray?"

"A woman, Anthony. It's another name for woman."

His father had died while Tony was in the service. He remembered when they called him in to tell him. He hadn't felt much. Startled, maybe, but not sad. It occurred to him that maybe the feeling would hit him later, but it never did. They had offered to send him home for the funeral, but he'd declined.

The next time he saw his mother was when he moved back in with her. Moving into his old room, which she had kept clean during his absence, was like stepping into the past. Life resumed its old shape, except for one major difference. The old man was gone.

His mother doted on him in a way she never had before, and Tony realized he had more or less stepped into his father's place. It was Tony his mother met at the door; it was he who sat at the head of the table. But doting meant more nagging, too: to do this, not to do that, to eat better, not to drink. Whatever. He couldn't satisfy her.

The first time he beat his mother up came after a

drinking spree. She had been sitting up, waiting for him, and when he got home immediately began to question him, treating him like some kid. He had hit her a couple of times.

And she had shut up. The next day he noticed she didn't nag him so much, yet still took care of him. To make up for hitting her, though neither of them mentioned it, he took her out to eat and to a movie, something the old man never did.

Tony wanted just to lie down on his bed and take a nap, to forget everything that had happened, but he shook off his lethargy, knowing he had to make some sort of plan. He had to fight passivity. It might be dangerous.

He stripped off his clothes, stepped into the stinging shower, and immediately began to feel some energy coming back into him. The water. It felt so good, purging him, clearing his mind.

"God, what a mess I'm in," he said. It all seemed to stem back to one little detail, to the fact that there was a miss in his car engine. Probably one dirty spark plug. Such was life that his fate would hinge on a piece of dirt. The miss in the engine had annoyed him, so he took the car to a garage to be worked on, then walked back to Shera's to borrow her car. She wasn't there—he'd known she wouldn't be—but he knew where she kept the spare key.

He planned to call on some customers, just an ordinary day, and then the kid darted out from nowhere, from between parked cars, just as they warn you about from the time you're the kid yourself till when you start driving. And it happened. He could still hear the thud. It was like seeing a movie in slow motion, the whole accident forever replaying, seeing that body thrown.

He drove around for a while, in a sort of daze, then found himself at home, as if it had been a magnet attracting him. He pulled the car into his mother's garage, where his car usually was, knowing she'd never look in there and wonder. It was not part of her territory; it was spidery.

He pulled the door shut and locked it.

And then there was Shera. Somehow, that didn't stick with him like the picture of the kid being thrown.

He toweled off in the shower, shaved, then took clean clothes out of the closet. As he pulled the contents from the pockets of yesterday's jeans, the insurance card fell to the floor. He picked it up and examined it.

Christ Almighty, he thought, Dallas. The name Laura was written across the top of the card in Shera's constricted handwriting. Now he knew where he had to start.

9

"I've got a grilled cheese ready for you, Tony," his mother said through the door.

It was the other Tony, the charming one, who emerged from the bedroom; she could feel it.

"You must be feeling better," she remarked.

He put his arm around her and ushered her down the hall. "I'm feeling fine, Mama. Who wouldn't be, with a mama to fix them some lunch?" He gave her shoulder a little squeeze. It made her feel good, to have him like this.

If only he would just start staying home nights again. It would be so nice. Then she wouldn't have the lonely times, wondering what every little sound was.

She got Tony settled at the table, then brought him the sandwich and some potato chips. "I'll get some bread and butter pickles for you. I bought the kind you like last time I was at the market."

Tony began to eat while she made another trip to the refrigerator.

"Mama, while you're up, will you get me some water?"

When she had brought him the glass of water, she sat down across the table and watched him.

"You look nice, Sonny." He was wearing a blue oxford cloth shirt and gray slacks.

"Thanks, Mama. Listen, I need some money. Just for a while. You got some in the sugar bowl?" He leaned forward and looked up under his eyelashes at her.

She frowned. "Well, I hate to use that money. It's for an emergency." She meant if the banks all failed or some other cataclysmic event.

"Mama, how much have you got in there?"

"Three hundred and fifty-four dollars."

"Well, I need it bad."

"What's the matter?"

"Nothing. I just need some money. C'mon, Mama."

She might as well get it for him, she thought, since he knew where she kept it and he would just take it anyway.

She pulled the bowl out of the cabinet with a sigh and drew the crumpled bills from it. Now she knew why he had turned on his charm. Oh, well, she thought, her reluctance disappearing, replaced by a feeling of satisfaction, that's what I'm for—to help him when he needs me.

Tony had finished his sandwich and was wiping his face with the napkin as she handed him the money.

"That's my girl," he said as he took it. Simultaneously, the cat leaped into his lap. "Christ," he said, jumping up, almost upsetting his chair, "she scared the shit out of me."

"Tony, your language," his mother admonished.

"Keep that damn cat out of my way," he said, making a pass at the cat with his foot. The cat nimbly sidestepped away from it.

The warmth that Mrs. Longoria was feeling about having him home, about helping him out when he needed it, vanished. "Don't hurt Miss Kitty, Sonny." She scooped the cat up and held it to her bosom, cooing to it.

He gave her a disgusted look, then disappeared down the hall.

"Where are you going?" she asked after him.

He ignored her and went into his room. A little while later, as she was cleaning up the dishes, she heard his door open. She tried to talk to him as he went by the kitchen, but he paid no attention and hurried out the front door. She noticed he was carrying a small suitcase.

10

As Lora waited during her call to the police department, she'd run across some notes in her basket on pending cases. On top was the one she'd ended rather abruptly to pursue Brad on break the day before. Now she scanned it, remembering that the woman—a Shera Johnson—was going to call her back after reporting her missing car to the police. She dialed the number, wondering why the woman hadn't returned the call. Probably had gotten cold feet about going to the police.

That poor thing had sounded so uncertain on the phone, Lora thought, like she needed a friend, confiding how she'd quit her job because it was so rough waiting on people and how she didn't like being on her feet so long.

And there I was, Lora thought, all self-absorbed, hurrying the timid little thing off the phone so I could play my own personal games, chasing Brad.

She felt guilty about being abrupt and wished she had been a little more sympathetic. Maybe she could assuage her conscience now. Sometimes Lora felt a claims person was more of a counselor than anything else, the way they listened to people's troubles. Not that the company encouraged the human angle. Efficiency was a "thou shalt," and it didn't include taking much extra time to be a listening ear, though most of the reps sacrificed a little efficiency for sympathy. They weren't the reps, however, who got the biggest merit increases. Only statistics counted for merit.

The phone rang twice, then was picked up. "Yeah?" a voice said. She identified herself, but before she could continue, the party on the opposite end hung up on her. Maybe I got a wrong number, she thought. She dialed again and decided she was right about the wrong number, because this time no one answered. Some people were so rude. They could have told her of her mistake, not just slammed the phone down. She put the paper back in the basket. Shera Johnson would have to make the next contact, if she got around to it.

11

Tony approached Shera's apartment warily, but nothing seemed to be out of the ordinary. He would just go in, check the place out, make sure there were no signs of his ever having been there. Simple.

As he passed the landlady's apartment, she popped out of the door, as if she had been waiting there. Tony didn't even acknowledge her presence with a grunt, but it irritated him that she had seen him. She could connect him with the place today. She didn't know his name, though.

The phone rang just as he got beside it, startling him. His nerves were taut. He automatically answered it. "Hello?"

"This is Lora with the Unified Assurance Company of America. Is Ms. Johnson in?"

Tony slammed the receiver down. His hands were shaking as he stood staring at the phone. Why in the hell did I answer that? he wondered. I'm not going to get out of this if I don't use my brain.

Quickly, he made a survey of the apartment. There was very little of his there, just a few items; a safety razor which could have been Shera's; a pair of underwear, wadded up and forgotten in a corner of the closet; a picture of him in Shera's billfold. He also withdrew the money, Shera's last pay, from the wallet. As he started to close her purse, he noticed a napkin with three words scribbled on it: precinct, case, officer. He frowned. He knew what it suggested—that she had called the police. He stuffed it into his pocket. A few other personal items in the apartment, not even a grocery bag full, were all that remained of his connection to Shera. He hurriedly emptied the contents of the ashtrays into the toilet and flushed them away.

He made another tour of the apartment with a wet cloth, wiping all the flat, plain surfaces where he thought the cops might try to lift fingerprints, especially the refrigerator and its shelves. How long did he have, he nervously wondered, before the body was found? After taking one last look around, he picked up the bag he'd been filling and the suitcase he'd brought with him and left for good, locking the door behind him.

12

Bill Graham pulled out the statement he'd taken from Shera Johnson and rubbed his forehead as he looked through it. He needed to think about this systematically. She had reported her car stolen. There were two possibilities: a—that the person this Montgomery woman heard was somehow mixed up with the thief, in which case he was no further along than before, or b—that the Johnson woman had a man in the picture about whom she hadn't told Bill, and the case would crack wide open. There was also the possibility that the overheard assault didn't have anything to do with this particular case at all. Bill sighed.

His mind seemed unwilling to concentrate on Ms. Johnson. Instead he smiled to himself, thinking about that soft southern accent he had just heard on the phone. He glanced at the paper on which he had written the name and phone number. Lora Montgomery. Her voice reminded him of his ex-wife, Marianne. She was a southerner, and he loved the way her words hung in the air after she said them. Time was no object to her in getting something said.

"What are you grinning about?" his partner, Dellasega, said, coming into the room.

"Daydreaming. Hey, let's go over to that Shera Johnson's house, the one with the missing car like the hit-and-run vehicle, and check her out. Maybe the neighbors know something. I just took a report from an insurance claims rep who got a call from a woman who mentioned a hit-and-run. Then the rep heard the caller being beaten up. Maybe she was the woman—"

Dellasega wasn't following. "Run that by again?"

Bill explained Lora's call.

"Yeah, let's go over," Dellasega agreed. "Sounds like a great idea, gives me a good excuse to put off typing this up." He waved a sheaf of papers. "What do they think I am, a goddamn typist?" he muttered, and threw the papers onto his desk.

Bill smiled. Dellasega was mouthy, but he was good-hearted. They had only been together a couple of weeks, but he thought it was going to be a good combination—Dellasega's volatility counterpointing his own stability.

He fell back into his reverie on the way to Shera Johnson's, thinking about Marianne and how it had all fallen apart after eighteen years. She wasn't going to be married to the police department any longer, she had said.

There didn't seem to be any choice, really. He could have quit his job, but then he would have been unhappy. What did she want him to do? Be a security guard? Push a broom somewhere? What did he really know but police work? He had been a waiter once.

Maybe he'd been ready for a change, too, if you got right down to it. When they married he would have taken any job just to have had her. He kind of felt that way again, after being single for a year, but Marianne had already found someone else. A real estate broker on Long Island.

Bill was curious about where Marianne had found him. The guy seemed to have lots of money, and they were already talking marriage. Bill recalled that it had taken him two years to get around to talking marriage to Marianne, after meeting her in a neighborhood café where he was working in the evenings while he went to school at NYU days. But she hadn't been in a hurry either. She had come to New York straight out of high school to be an actress. She would come in with other theatre hopefuls, and it got to be their regular hangout. Most of them were in shows on and off. When they found out that Bill, the waiter, was a student, he got to be their friend and eventually her lover.

When Bill finished school he owed the Army some time, and Marianne—maybe not wanting to be left behind—got pregnant, though she always maintained it was an accident. So they married. She was ready for a hiatus in her acting career, and it didn't matter anyway, because he loved her dearly and the marriage and baby were just the natural course of things. So was a fiftieth anniversary, grandkids, growing wrinkled and gray together, he thought. That's the way his parents did it. He had assumed his life would follow much the same pattern. But it hadn't. The eventual career he chose, and perhaps the mood of the times, sidetracked his domestic life.

He sighed and Dellasega glanced over at him.

"You okay?" he asked.

Bill nodded. "I think I need a vacation." What he didn't need were thoughts about Marianne. Better to think about that soft voice on the phone. He would check this lead out, then give her a call back, maybe talk to her awhile. After all, he had some time off coming, and a brother in Waxahachie, Texas, not far from Dallas at all.

You jerk, he told himself. Pretty hard up, aren't you? A city full of women and you want to go after someone in Dallas. Probably married, too. You're just putting off a need to find another woman, so you pick someone unattainable, someone halfway across the country, for God's sake, and you don't have to do much about it. You can sit around home mooning, and not admit that dating scares the hell out of you at your age.

Maybe that wasn't all there was to it, though. After all, he did appreciate southern women, like Marianne. They seemed feminine and vulnerable. They weren't necessarily so, but he liked the illusion they presented. He figured a psychologist could make something out of that. Did he need to feel powerful? Was that why he as a cop as well? He didn't think so—at least it didn't seem to come out that way in his work. He shrugged his introspectiveness off, figuring that delving into his psyche wouldn't help anything. He and Dellasega had work to do.

13

Louella French heard quick but heavy footsteps coming down the stairs, so she put down the afghan she was crocheting for her sister's girl and stepped over to the door of the apartment. Peering through the eyehole, she saw the boyfriend go by again, then waited till she heard the outer door close.

Mr. French was long in his grave, and his widow had little to do but crochet and listen to the comings and goings of her tenants, and their friends, too, for that matter. Little missed her attention, and she noticed what a short time the boyfriend had stayed just now. Another thing she had noticed was that Shera hadn't left for work that morning at her usual time. Something was going on; she felt it, and she trusted her instincts. She undid the security chain on her door, opened it and stepped out into the hallway.

She saw the boyfriend on the street, getting into a cab, and frowned. She'd never seen him leave in a taxi before. What was he carrying in that bag? He'd carried a suitcase in, which he still had, but he hadn't had the bag. She watched the cab pull away.

The landlady started up the stairs. Outside the door, she paused to catch her breath. Then she knocked. No one answered. She knocked again, insistently, and when there was still no answer, shook her head. "Why didn't I bring up the extra key?" she mumbled. "Louella French, you don't have the sense you were born with." She had expected to find Shera at home.

She kept duplicate keys on a board next to the door, shaped like a fish. Each one hung from a cup hook. Her boy had made the board long ago in a woodworking class in high school. When she got back downstairs, she plucked the key to Shera's apartment off the board, then started the laborious climb again. "Getting my exercise today," she muttered.

She wondered when Shera could have left that morning, deciding she must have surely been late to work. "Place is probably a mess," she said, expecting the worst when she unlocked the door and peeped in to make sure the coast was clear. "Miss Johnson?" she said tentatively. "You in here?"

She entered, her gaze sweeping the living room and noticing nothing out of order. She took a mental inventory of the furnishings, then went over and scrutinized the couch for cigarette burns, remembering the man in 2A who had almost burned the building down one time when he fell asleep with a cigarette.

She hated to admit it, but the place looked good, even clean. She ran her finger across the coffee table and inspected it. Shera didn't strike her as such a tidy housekeeper as this. Her gaze turned to the kitchenette. She went over and opened a cabinet. It was almost empty. The trash container was full of jars. She suddenly had the sneaking suspicion that Shera was getting ready to move out without any notice. That might explain *his* bag, too.

Good thing I have the deposit, she thought.

Her attention turned to the shelves stashed between the refrigerator and the stove. She was puzzled about why they were out of the refrigerator. Frowning again, she reached out to open the door.

14

The scream reached Graham and Dellasega just when they had gotten to the second landing, and they broke into a run, taking the stairs two at a time. They burst into the apartment, ready for anything, and found Mrs. French hospital white, silent after her initial shriek, but with mouth still agape, hands cradling her face.

They took the scene in swiftly. What had been a routine connection between the timid person who had come in to report the missing car and the Montgomery woman's phone call had turned into something more.

"Call in," Graham told Dellasega as he pulled the victim's eyelid open. The eye was beginning to look leathery. Rigor mortis hadn't set in, but the body had a pasty white cast. "Get the lab boys over here." He quickly shoved the refrigerator door shut against the grotesque sight of the body.

Mrs. French had found her voice again. "It's horrid, just horrid," her voice shrilly announced.

"Do you know her?"

"Yes, she's my tenant, Miss Johnson," she said, her

voice starting at a normal pitch but sliding perilously upward again. "It must have been her boyfriend. I've never felt comfortable about him. He was too pretty. Everything's too easy for that type." Her speech was accelerating, threatening hysterics.

Graham ushered her over to the couch, out of sight of the refrigerator, and gently urged her to sit down.

"Hadn't we better call the police?" she fluttered.

"We are the police, m'am, plainclothes." Graham pulled out his identification and showed it to her. "I need to ask you a few questions. Shera Johnson. Was that her name?" He took his notebook out.

She nodded her assent.

"May I have your name, please?"

"Louella French, and this is my building. I'm the landlady."

This might be easy, Graham thought. Some people you asked a question, you got a simple answer; others opened up like a spigot. Then you just had to sort out fact from opinion.

"How long has she lived here?"

"Six months."

"About the boyfriend. Do you know his name?"

"No—oh, let me see. It seems like I know his first name, if I could only think of it. Oh, this is so awful—I may never be able to rent this apartment again after something like this."

"I don't think that'll be a problem, m'am; apartments are hard to come by. When was the last time you saw her alive?"

Her voice quavered as she said, "Well, let me see. It was yesterday. I met her coming in from the store."

"She was coming in from the store?"

"No, I was. I don't know where she was coming in from. I met her on the street. It must have been near five."

Graham realized that was when Shera Johnson would have been returning from her trip to the precinct house. "What about next of kin? Do you know if she had any relatives in the city?"

The landlady shook her head. "She was kind of close-mouthed. I always try to get acquainted with my tenants, but she seemed kind of rabbity, if you know what I mean. Hard to get to know."

He tried to get more information, but there appeared to be little the woman knew about the victim. The sound of a siren coming near effectively put a halt to the questioning. Graham stood up and went over to where Dellasega stood by the refrigerator.

"Gross, huh?" Dellasega said.

Graham nodded. Here was a dead girl who just yesterday had walked meekly into the station. It couldn't help but take some feeling out of a man, seeing this sort of thing day in and day out. Little affected him anymore. He got more tears in his eyes when they played "The Star Spangled Banner" at a baseball game than he did from the stuff of real life. He needed to try to find some empathy in himself. It seemed to be drained dry; he had drunk to the bottom of the glass during his first years on the force, and all that remained at the bottom was an ironic concern about not being affected by the rot of human nature he saw daily.

Marianne had agreed. She told him he was a nonfeeling bastard. He frowned at the memory of tiny, but spunky, Marianne spouting the words at him.

Glad for the distraction, he walked over to the door to meet the other police personnel who had just come on the scene. Self-reflection was always threatening; it might confirm what one feared—that one was, what? Unlovable?

The police had gone over the apartment for fingerprints, looked for any other evidence, and searched for information about the victim, but so far the place looked as if it had been wiped clean. Meanwhile, Mrs. French had gone down to her own apartment.

A short time later Graham had followed and knocked on her door. "May I ask you a few more questions?" he said when she answered.

"Oh, certainly, officer. Come in." She had calmed down, here in the security of her own apartment. She offered him a cup of coffee, which he accepted. "It's decaf. I just can't seem to sleep nights if I drink regular coffee."

No wonder, Graham thought when he took the first sip, if this is any indication. It was the thickest coffee he had had in ages.

It was her turn to ask a question: Why were the police on the scene when she screamed?

Graham told her enough to satisfy her.

"Tony," she suddenly said.

Graham squinted his eyes and looked at her quizzically.

"That was the boyfriend's name. I knew it would come to me. I've heard her yell it after him as he'd leave."

"Did they fight?"

"Did they fight? It was more like he knocked her around, then she whined after him to come back when he'd storm out of there. She seemed so quiet when I rented the place to her, but you just can't ever tell. The boyfriend was the trouble. And he used some pretty bad language, let me tell you. What some women put up with." She gave a disgusted snort.

Graham took a sip of his coffee, hoping she would continue.

"When he left today, he was quiet enough, though," she said, "but then, of course, he didn't have anyone to yell at anymore, did he? He took care of that."

Graham leaned toward the woman intently. "He was here today?"

"Why, yes. Just about five minutes before you came."

15

Tony felt fortunate to get a place on a flight to Dallas. He tried to be inconspicuous, not wanting anyone to notice him, but every time he looked up, the young woman who had given him his boarding pass was looking at him. The muscle at the corner of Tony's mouth began its nervous twitch. He felt as if at any moment he would see a swarm of police coming down the concourse. He was relieved when they finally called his flight and he was safely on board.

His only luggage was the small suitcase, which he carried on with him. It contained two extra shirts, a pair of slacks, several changes of underwear, and socks.

He handed the hostess his boarding pass and she directed him to the back of the plane, the smoking section. He put the valise in the compartment above the seat, then moved to the place by the window. He didn't like flying;

he was already getting nervous, and by the time they began their taxi down the runway for takeoff, he was gripping the arm of the chair.

A fat man seated in the same row noticed. "Don't like to fly?"

Tony shook his head.

"Hoo boy, I love it," the man said as they gathered speed. "They could fly me to the moon. You look a little green around the gills, though. Need you a drink; that'll help."

They were off the ground, climbing, circling. Tony sighed, relieved that the plane had ceased to rattle and groan as if it were on its last legs.

"Scotch and water," he told the hostess, knowing it would make him feel better.

A few hours and as many drinks later they dropped down at Lambert Field in St Louis through a rainstorm, but Tony tolerated the landing with alcoholic equanimity. The fat man and Tony stayed aboard. A new group of passengers boarded, including a well-built middle-aged man in blue jeans and a cowboy shirt, who stopped at their aisle. He sat down next to the fat man.

While waiting for the plane to taxi, Tony had the uncomfortable feeling that someone was looking at him, Glancing across the aisle, he saw that the newcomer, in fact, was staring. Nor did the man look away when Tony caught him at it. The look had an invitation in it, the kind you expect occasionally with the opposite sex.

Tony was used to it. His good, almost effeminate looks and his well-developed body caught the attention not only of women, but also of homosexual men. And in spite of this guy's straight appearance, Tony was sure he was gay because of the way he was eyeing him.

When no one else sat down near Tony, the man moved across the aisle to sit next to him. Just as he did, the seat belt sign went on.

"Hi. I'm Bart. What's your name?" He put his hand across to Tony.

"Joe Thomas." His father's two given names. Tony didn't offer to shake hands.

"You live in Dallas?" Bart drawled, withdrawing his hand.

"No, New York."

"Gonna be in Dallas long?"

"No." Tony was keeping his answers curt, not wanting to encourage the guy, but after a few more questions he said, "Listen, why don't you just move your ass back to your own seat?"

"Can't during takeoff," Bart said smugly.

The hostesses went through their routine once the seat belt light went off, then Tony said, "Now there's nothing to stop you." Bart pointed out affably that the fat man opposite them was spread out over three seats and already had his eyes shut as if for a nap. "Shouldn't disturb him; wouldn't be neighborly. Listen, why don't I buy you a drink?"

Tony shrugged. He could use another drink and he hated to spend any more of his money. He might need it. So when the hostess came by with their two drinks, he didn't object when Bart paid.

The more he thought about it, maybe Bart was the perfect foil. Maybe he had been dropped here by fate for Tony to use. All Tony had to do was wangle an invitation, and then he would have the perfect place to stay in Dallas. No motels, no restaurants. And he didn't think there would be much wangling to do. The only question was, once wangled, could he keep the guy at bay for a few days, till he took care of business and fled?

"Ahhh," Bart sighed, after his first swig. "One of the finer libations." He paused, then asked, "Have you been to Dallas before?"

"No. Are you a native?"

"Yep. Well, not of Dallas. I was born in East Texas. In the piney woods."

"I thought Texas didn't have any trees."

"Texas has a little of everything. We have our own writers, our own music." He stopped a moment, took a drink, then asked, "Say, you like Willie Nelson?"

Tony shrugged. "He's okay."

"You're probably a hard rock man. Well, I heard Willie play in person when he had short hair and wore a suit—over in Fort Worth. We have our own food, too. Boy, would I like to feed you a bowl of my chili; it'd blow your socks off. Maybe while you're down here you could come by and I'd fix you some." He took a last swallow of his drink. "You coming down here on business?"

Tony nodded.

"Meeting someone?"

"No. Just a few days there, then back to New York."

"I could show you around. I mean, you can't have business all the time. All work and no play, you know." He laughed heartily, then looked right at Tony. "I'd like to show you around; I know Dallas like the back of my hand."

Tony gave him a tentative little smile and gazed at him from under his lashes, as he did with women. "I guess that would be okay. But I don't know where I'm going to be staying."

"Shoot, why don't you stay at my place? I've fixed me

up this old house. It's about eighty years old and it's a beaut. Put in some stained glass, and I stripped all the old finish off the woodwork.'' Bart launched into a full-scale description of his labors on the house.

Tony wasn't remotely interested, but he pretended he was, nodding appropriately. He glanced out the window at one point and saw that the rain clouds had dissipated, their place taken by clouds that looked like puffs of meringue on top of a pudding. ''How much further to Dallas?'' he asked when Bart paused for a breath.

''Another hour, I reckon.'' He glanced at his watch, then looked around to the back of the cabin. ''Think I'll make a little trip to the boy's room. Don't take any wooden nickels while I'm gone,'' he told Tony as he stood up stiffly and started down the aisle.

Oh, God, Tony thought. Will I be able to stand this? He decided to feign sleep upon Bart's return. And it worked. His seat companion took an airline magazine out of the pocket on the seat in front and began to read.

Feigning soon turned to the real thing. Tony fell into a sleep troubled by a dream of driving an old car that he had owned about ten years earlier. He was driving in the mountains, something he'd never done in real life. Near the summit the car lost power and began slowly to start moving backward down the incline. He clamped on the brakes, but his foot went almost to the floor before there was any resistance at all to the pressure and the car itself hardly reacted at all. His momentum began to increase until the car was careening at breakneck speed, with Tony trying to steer while looking back over his shoulder. Sweat poured off him; his eyes ached as he strained to turn them farther in their sockets. He had to get turned around; he was coming to a hairpin curve. At the last moment he executed a bootlegger turn, spinning the car around. It rocked perilously near the edge of the mountainside, but he jerked the wheel and pulled it to the other side. Too far. He was rushing toward a wall of rock . . .

Just then he felt someone shaking him by the knee. "Gotta fasten up now," a strange voice said. It took him a moment to remember where he was.

The captain came on the speaker. "We're beginning our descent to Dallas-Fort Worth International. The temperature in the greater metropolitan area is seventy-five degrees. It promises to be a fantastic evening in the land of the Cowboys. Hope you enjoy it. We've enjoyed having you aboard."

Tony moved his seat to the erect position, then fastened his seat belt.

"This is really your lucky day," Bart said as they waited in the line-up of people to get off the plane. "My car is in long-term parking, so you won't have to deal with public transportation."

Tony nodded, wondering, though, about this arrangement he had made. He could almost hear a mental tape recorder with his father's voice deriding him for the company he was about to keep.

He tried to look inconspicuous, hanging close to Bart and talking to him, just so he wouldn't stand out as being alone. But every time a security guard came near, he felt uneasy. He was relieved when Bart's bags finally appeared and they could find the car and start for Dallas.

Space was what Tony noticed. Even though the skyline was riddled with high rises, there was space. Everything wasn't crammed together, as in New York City. And new.

The whole place suggested the space age to Tony. Glass and chromelike steel everywhere. Buildings that reflected the dying day in their windows.

Bart insisted on driving Tony by the Texas School Depository from which Lee Harvey Oswald had shot Kennedy. "This is the thing everyone wants to see when they come to Dallas." Tony didn't feel even vaguely interested; he'd only been a little boy when the assassination happened, and he had more important things to think about now.

There was a seamier side of town, some of which they drove through to get to Bart's house. They pulled into a driveway, surrounded by what to Tony was a huge yard. Two gigantic oak trees dressed the front yard in deep shade, even though it wasn't late and they had picked up an hour flying west. The setting looked like an illustration out of a grade-school reader.

And there was still more space, Tony noted. Everything had space around it. Land had been cheap, and there had been lots of it when these houses were built. The house itself was big. A two-story frame. Green shingle roof. Gas light in front.

They parked next to the side door, which went into the kitchen. "Is that you, Bart?" someone shouted. A slender man—the same physical type as Tony—came in to greet them.

"Hi, Lon," Bart said. He set his bags down. "Lonnie, this is Joe. Joe, Lonnie."

Lonnie's left eyebrow shot up critically. "Well, where did you pick him up?" he said caustically.

"Don't be bitchy. Joe is here on business and I promised to show him around. He's going to stay here."

"Oh, glory," Lonnie said, and flounced back into the living room.

"Don't mind him," Bart said, picking up his bag again. "He just gets jealous. C'mon, I'll show you your room."

Tony had remained silent during this whole interchange. Now he said, "Hey, maybe I'd better find a motel."

"Oh, shee-it." He divided the expletive into two syllables, Texas style. "Don't be turned off by him."

"Wait a minute, here. Remember—I'm not turned on. You got that straight?"

Bart laughed. "I've got that—straight." He opened the swinging door into the living room for Tony.

Lonnie had hung a Welcome Home sign in the living room, with several balloons at either end. "That's what you been up to," Bart said. "Thanks, buddy."

Lonnie sat draped over a couch in the center of the living room. "I didn't expect you to bring company."

"It was an impulse."

"You and your impulses."

"Hey, we're hungry. Would you start to rustle up some grub while I show Joe a room?"

"I suppose."

Bart took Tony upstairs, and after depositing his own bags in his room, opened another door for Tony. "Here you go."

The room was straight out of some decorator magazine, Tony thought. The bedspread, curtains, and wallpaper all matched, in a big bold floral print. The brass bed had four pillows at the head, covered with a ruffly thing. A ruffly cover disguised a table by the bed. A white wicker rocker sat by the window.

"This is the guest room. Sorry it's so feminine. Lonnie's a decorator; he did the whole house for me. It's not something I would have done, but it's nice, I think. You know, it kind of looks like quality, like someone took some time on it. I think that's important." He paused. "Towels and washcloths are in the closet in the bathroom. Now just make yourself at home. You can come on back down now, or rest up before we eat. Later, we can take you on a tour of Dallas."

16

All the early shift reps were doing their last minute tasks, a few still stuck with clients on the phones. The western reps still had another two hours to work. Lora saw Brad approaching as she put the last few papers into her desk.

"Ready to go?" he asked as he drew near.

"Sure am," Lora said, a bit nervously, glancing at her watch. "Just let me get my desk locked." It was still a few minutes before five, her quitting time.

Sue, watching what was going on from two desks away, noticed Lora's reluctance to leave a few moments early. "Go on," she said, "I'll catch any last minute calls."

"Thanks," Lora replied, turning the key in the lock. She dropped the keys into her purse and stood up, the soft gathers of her skirt hugging her thighs provocatively, a fact not lost on Brad. She was glad she had worn this silky-looking dress today. She thought she looked good in it, but more important, she felt good in it. Its aqua color was one which, she had read somewhere, flattered any coloring. It didn't hurt, either, that the divorce had trimmed about ten pounds off her weight. Her size had never been a problem, but time had been adding a pound or so a year, particularly in her thighs and hips. Now she was back to a svelte size eight.

"We've got a problem with two cars," Brad said when they reached the parking lot. "Why don't we leave yours here and I'll bring you back later."

"You sure it won't be out of your way?"

He shrugged. "No matter." He was steering Lora toward his car by the elbow. She was glad he'd insisted, because it would be nice to be driven somewhere for a change. One of the things she missed since her divorce was someone else taking charge, doing the driving.

Brad led her to a sporty-looking car, putting her ten-year-old heap of junk to shame. Once inside, he leaned one forearm on the steering wheel and turned toward her.

"Well, what do you think? Where shall we go?"

"I don't care."

Brad turned on the ignition. "Well, how about the Italian Gardens. It's one of my favorites. But first let's stop and have a drink somewhere," he suggested. "It's too early to eat. Okay?" The engine purred to a start.

"Sure." She certainly didn't want to get home at seven o'clock, all ready for a big evening, as usual, in front of her TV.

17

Bill Graham thought he ought to tell Lora Montgomery in Dallas that there had been a murder. After all, it looked as if the victim was the woman she had heard being beaten up. They had found a Unified Assurance policy in a dresser drawer, which made that possibility even more likely. He didn't admit it to himself, but the fact that he wanted to hear Lora's voice again came into play, too.

He dialed the number she had given him.

"Claims, Sue speaking."

"Lora Montgomery, please."

"I'm sorry, but she's gone for the day. May I help you?"

"No, I need to reach her." He felt a wave of momentary disappointment which surprised him. "Do you have her home phone number?"

"I'm sorry but I'm not authorized to give that out. May I take your number and have her return your call tomorrow?"

He identified himself and asked that she do that. Bill was surprised when Sue called him back in just a few minutes.

"Listen," she said, "I just wanted to verify that you were really calling from the police. Now I can give you her number."

"Good. She had contacted me about a call she received and I'm following through on it. Do you happen to know if I can reach her at home this evening?"

"As a matter of fact, she has a date tonight, so she may be hard to catch."

Which turned out to be a true statement. He had been off duty for a couple of hours, but he hated to go home, so he sat there and caught up on some paperwork and tried the phone number several times, but didn't get an answer. He stuck her number in his shirt pocket, thinking he would try again later.

He sauntered down the street, stopping in at a deli for supper. Morton, the shop's owner, greeted Bill when he came in.

"The usual?"

"Am I that predictable?" Bill asked, smiling.

"Yep. Always on Tuesday it's pastrami on rye with potato salad."

"Sounds good to me." He stood by the counter while Morton put the sandwich together, a big delectable thing a person could hardly get his mouth around.

"You look a little tired tonight."

"Yeah. I feel kind of dragged out."

"You need to have some fun, get out and kick up your heels. One of these days you'll be getting married again, but while you're single you ought to live it up a little, you know?"

Bill laughed. "That's easy for you married guys to say. If you were single, you'd still be in here working sixty-hour weeks, the same as usual. More, probably."

Morton shrugged and squirted some oil on the sandwich to make it juicier.

Bill watched, a passing thought about his cholesterol level surfacing momentarily, then said, "I was thinking today, though, maybe I oughta find myself a girlfriend."

"I got a niece, newly divorced, about your age."

"No, thanks, Morton." Bill chuckled. "No one newly divorced. She's probably hot to get remarried. I'm not ready for that."

"You could be right." He handed Bill the sandwich. "Want a coffee?"

"Yeah, please. I need someone who's had time to get their feet back on solid earth again."

"Well, at least you're thinking about it. That's a good sign."

"I guess," he said. Another customer had come in, so Bill left the counter and sat down at one of the three tables in the place.

Lora Montgomery—actually just her voice, the softness of it—had had a big effect on him. Funny. She made him want to find someone.

He searched his mind, trying to think of somebody he might call.

The walk home was pleasant. The weather was perfect for springtime, although they were predicting rain. He let himself into his basement apartment, one he'd taken after the divorce. For the first six months he hadn't done anything to it; he had used it like a motel room. Then one day he saw a framed poster in a shop and it had appealed to him. It showed the United States as viewed, chauvinistically, from New York City. New York filled up the entire foreground, and there was not much else except the west coast. It now graced the wall behind the couch. Next he had bought a schefflera and a big basket in which to put the pot. Before he knew it, the apartment was beginning to look decorated. He added mini-blinds because he liked the way they looked in other people's places, then a rag rug, although the word rag was sort of a misnomer when he considered the price tag.

About the time he got it looking the way he wanted, he decided he was over the worst part of the divorce. He was mending, and the apartment decorating had helped.

At the sound of the key, his cat, Sam, came scampering to the door, meowing. Sam, too, had helped him regain his equilibrium. A neighbor had moved out while Sam was out tomcatting around for several weeks. "Please," she had said, "when he comes back, please take care of him."

Bill, who had never liked cats, promised, thinking that the cat had probably come to no good end and wouldn't ever return. But one night he heard a meowing at the door and it was Sam. He let him in and Sam had been a regular fixture ever since. He liked the cat's independence, yet he found that the old fellow had a distinct personality, something he never attributed to cats. He was more like a dog, in Bill's opinion. Of course, he had never been around a cat before. Sam had been with him over a year now, and Bill would miss him if he were gone.

He scratched Sam behind the ears, then tried calling Lora Montgomery—to tell her about the woman—but no one answered. Just as he hung up, he noticed that Sam had jumped into the schefflera and was scratching the dirt.

"Out of there, you cotton-pickin' cat," he shouted, using one of Marianne's expressions. He started toward Sam, rattling a newspaper, and the cat jumped out and raced behind the couch in mock fear.

The best thing about Sam, besides the fact that he was someone to take care of, was that he was someone to talk to, Bill thought. Otherwise, after work he'd never hear the sound of his own voice. Sam helped remind him that there was an outer life, as well as an inner one, whenever he began to feel isolated.

18

Brad maneuvered the car out of the parking space to the parking lot exit. Silently he sped to the freeway and bullied his way onto 635 going east, fitting smoothly into the flow of traffic once on, but not being content with that. He gunned the car and darted in and out of traffic.

"I know a nice little place over on Upper Greenville," he said, not really expecting Lora's opinion. Lora was holding onto the seat by the time they wheeled into the parking lot.

The dark-paneled interior of the bar was dimly lit, a shadowy contrast to the daylight outside. The place was quiet, the sounds muffled by carpet and acoustic ceiling. A bearded piano player glanced up from his soft-pedaled music and nodded. He was improvising skillfully, not interfering with the few conversations going on around the room.

A waitress—a young, curvaceous redhead—approached them as soon as they were seated. She had on tight, shiny black slacks and a black turtleneck. "What would you all like?" she drawled, focusing entirely on Brad.

After giving her a blatant once-over, Brad turned to Lora and raised his eyebrows questioningly.

"I'd like white wine," she said.

"Wellers and water for me. And a telephone." His eyes cursorily searched the room.

"Over behind the bar," she said.

"I'm going to make reservations for dinner," Brad told Lora, excusing himself.

Lora sat there alone, rolling up the corners of her paper cocktail napkin. Now that they were together, a situation she had only fantasized about, she wondered how the reality would match up. The fantasy had been a nebulous thing, not mapped out specifically, and now she was confronted with the prospect of several hours to fill. What would they talk about? Somehow she felt that the burden of entertainment, the weight of seeing that things proceeded smoothly, was her responsibility. Feeling uneasy, she wondered if she could hold his interest when he obviously had his choice of many single women at the office—younger women.

She felt a bit foolish all of a sudden, being out with him, but there seemed so few men, single ones her own age. Married men stayed married until they found someone worth getting a divorce over, a catalyst, and then they remarried very quickly. That was the pattern she'd noticed. But women divorced because the marriage had become intolerable. Usually no one was waiting in the wings; consequently there were more single women floating around unattached. She had thought Martin was going to follow the pattern, but he hadn't. But that was Martin—he was nothing if not atypical. Just when you expected him to behave in a certain way, he didn't.

She watched Brad at the phone. He was watching the woman at the bar. That and his blatant sizing up of the waitress while on a first date didn't appear very promising. He would be impossible over the long haul, Lora thought. But who was she trying to kid? She had known that before she accepted the date, hadn't she?

Martin hadn't been like Brad. His eyes had always been for her. Or so it had seemed. That's why it had been such a surprise when he came in one night and announced that he wanted a divorce. He'd been late, and she was already in bed. He'd been working late often, but she never once doubted that he was indeed working. She had the comfort of naiveté.

She had greeted him sleepily and watched him take off his tie and jacket in the light from the closet. Then he announced it, out of the blue.

At first she thought he was kidding. But when she saw he was serious, her question was, "Why?" followed by "Who?"

"It doesn't matter," he had replied.

"Doesn't matter? Of course it matters. You tell me you want a divorce, and the other person doesn't matter?"

She found out later, when she felt infinitely wiser about such things, that it really didn't matter. It could have been anyone. It turned out that the woman was a secretary at the manufacturing firm where Martin was an engineer. She had been divorced by her husband under similar circumstances. It was as if they were all caught up in a round robin—okay, everyone, move over one person. Except Lora's inability to find someone to get involved with had broken the chain. If someone had appeared at the right moment, she would have probably fallen into place.

Good conversations occur in the dark, and theirs had

lasted all night and seemed terribly rational; she felt as if it were a vigil for her marriage. But by morning the flaws in the night's reasoning stood exposed in the sharp light of day, and Lora, depressed, had to struggle to get ready to go to work.

Night after night, she would draw him into similar conversations, trying to grasp what was happening to them. But there seemed to be no truth; each hour of the day had a logic of its own. Finally, she was just plain worn down by exhaustion, or perhaps boredom, and she agreed to a divorce.

Her first reaction to the divorce itself had been a sense of failure. She'd muffed the two most important things a good middle-class Oklahoma girl could have out of life: marriage and family. It must have been a period of mourning; some days she would feel all right and think she was "well," then her loneliness would hit her again and she would feel she was drowning in the depths of depression. Finally, after a lengthy series of ups and downs, the decree was made and she began to heal, meaning she wasn't blaming herself so much.

Just after the divorce was final, Martin announced that he and his girlfriend weren't going to marry after all, and he started coming around to see Lora again. He called frequently, wanting to take her to dinner or come over and just be with her. Now he had a new girlfriend, but he still continued to come around.

She didn't usually encourage Martin's visits, because they confused her, but she did occasionally have dinner with him, when she was feeling lonely and he happened to call. He even talked about a reconciliation for a while, but she wasn't sure she could risk it emotionally. She did reflect on how her life had become awfully gray after the emotional tumult of the last year. Feast or famine, she thought.

Now, Brad returned to the table just as the waitress brought the drinks. "Dinner at seven," he said, glancing at his watch. "That gives us an hour." He took a sip of his drink. "Well, how is the claims business?"

"Same as usual. Sometimes I feel as if every car in the state of New York must be insured by us and is wrecked at least once a week."

"Ummm," he murmured through the drink. "Well, what was that weird one that had you so shook today?"

His question brought it abruptly back to her, but by now it seemed more like a dream than a reality, since the event itself was so dreamlike anyway. "Oh. Well, it sounded as if someone was getting beaten up." She related the first part of the call and how it had been terminated so abruptly. "I—I don't know what happened to her, but . . ." Lora rubbed the condensation on her glass with her forefinger. "There didn't seem to be anything for me to do."

"Did you get a name?" Brad's hand had reached over to nonchalantly trace the fingers of her hand. His touch was so electric to her that she lost her train of thought. "Uh . . . a name? No, I, uh . . . didn't," she said, trying to regain her composure. "All I know is it was in New York."

"Then I guess there's not much you can do except quit worrying about it."

She hadn't been worrying about it, not since he had asked her out, an effective stimulus for pushing everything else out of her head, and now she could hardly concentrate on the call at all. As she lifted her glass to her lips, she noticed she was trembling, as if she were terribly cold. Why was she so nervous?

They ordered another round, and by the time they left for dinner, she was feeling giddy and much more conversational. In fact, she was feeling like the world's most clever conversationalist.

The dinner was excellent, and they took their time over it. Lora learned that Brad lived on Lake Ray Hubbard, that the apartment complex had a swimming pool, tennis court, clubhouse, and sauna; that he had a catamaran at the boat dock. She learned that his apartment, his boat, his car, his pool, all were the best, better than anyone else's. Because Brad was careful about getting the best.

Despite all his hype, she was enjoying herself. The liquor had helped.

Just as she was taking another sip, Brad said, "You know, one of the nicest things about maturity is getting beyond games. I used to be so into them."

Lora almost choked on her drink. She grabbed her napkin and indecorously sputtered until she got her breath back.

"You okay?" Brad asked.

"Yes, yes," she sputtered. "Just swallowed wrong." She hid her mirth behind her napkin.

"I'll follow you home," Brad said as they reached the office parking lot where her car sat forlornly in the middle, all alone.

"Oh, that isn't necessary."

"I insist. I'm not going to leave you here."

It was settled. As she drove to her house, she debated about what was to follow. She decided to invite him in for a drink. After all, it was still early.

Brad stayed in sight in the rearview mirror. She led him

through a maze of turns to get to her street. When she pulled into the driveway, Brad drove in behind her and she walked back to his car.

"Want to come in for a drink," she asked.

He didn't hesitate. "Didn't know you were out in the country," he said as he got out of the car.

She followed his glance around. Though it was dark, one did get the impression of emptiness. None of the houses had any trees of appreciable size yet. And beyond? It was just open country. Very few lights twinkled in the distance. "Oh, you're further out than this," she replied.

"In miles, yes, but this has a lonely feel, looking off that way." He pointed beyond her house.

They walked to the porch, just a slab of concrete one step up, and he held the screen while she unlocked the front door.

"Well, this is it," she said; not the best or the biggest, she thought to herself. She swept her arm around after she flipped on the light switch which turned on the burgundy ginger-jar lamp beside the couch. "Home sweet home." The gesture took in the inexpensive off-white couch with its matching easy chair and ottoman, and the beige drapes bordering mini-blinds. The room was small but tasteful.

Brad made no comment. Instead he took her arm and pulled her to him. "I'm glad you led me here. I may never find my way back out, which may be all right."

She pulled away and said, "Two left turns and then a right. That's all you have to remember." She put her purse on the chair and went to the kitchen to mix drinks. "What would you like? I have gin, scotch, and vodka." She reached under the counter and opened the cabinet, pulling the bottles out, along with some mixes, trying subtly to dust them off, so they wouldn't look so unused.

He came in behind her as she put the bottles on the counter and took two glasses from the cabinet.

''I'll have you,'' he whispered into her ear, and slipped his arms around her, burying his face in her hair.

''Scotch and water okay?'' she asked breathlessly.

He mumbled his assent, so she poured the scotch, her hand shaking as she added the water, then turned around in his arms, leaning back against them, and handed him his drink. ''I hope it's the way you like it,'' she said, then added hesitantly, ''Ice?''

He took the drink, his eyes on hers, his mouth turned up in a slight smile. He half closed his eyelids, a look designed to make women melt, probably practiced in front of his mirror. And it was effective; at least her body responded, if her mind could just stop being so analytical, so rational. She kept seeing him as an observer would, the situation from afar, rather than as a participant.

''You're the way I like it,'' Brad murmured. He put down his drink and took hers and set it down, too. Then he pulled her closer and kissed her roughly, his tongue probing her mouth. She was responding, but she didn't want to, not this quickly. What did he mean to her anyway? Nothing. The sexual tension was almost unbearable. She was breathing hard, just being this close to him. His hand had gone up her back and he was unzipping her dress.

''Don't, Brad,'' she mumbled through the kiss, pushing his arms down. ''Not yet.'' This was an automatic verbal response programmed into her many years before.

''Mmm, come on, baby,'' he whispered, nibbling on her earlobe. His hand was inside the back of her dress.

She pulled away from him with effort and reached back to rezip her dress, then melted back into his arms, expecting him to kiss her again. But the rules had changed in the years since she had dated.

"Oh, shit, don't play that with me."

By now she knew she couldn't have the evening her way, with the romantic trappings of the past. But still she tried to salvage it.

"It's too soon, Brad. I guess I'm old-fashioned," she said, realizing as she spoke just how true it must be. "I want the romance." Was romance dead? she wondered. She could hear herself sounding so good. What was wrong with her? Wasn't a physical release what she wanted from him? Why back away from it now? Get on with it and get it over, this artificial virginal state.

She started to reach up and pull his hair away from his forehead, a gesture of tenderness, but he backed away from her, picked up his drink and took a quick shot, then put it back down on the counter.

"Listen, babe, I've seen the way you look at me from your desk. I know you want me, so let's not be coy. I told you I'm not into games."

Inwardly Lora cringed, knowing his observation was right. Had she been so obvious, mooning over him? Were her fellow workers laughing at her? So she struck back, out of her embarrassment. "Why, you egotistical bastard," she snapped at him. "I may want someone, but it isn't you."

"And it ain't gonna be, honey." He was at the door. "Go do yourself." He slammed the door behind him.

Lora was seething, partly because she was humiliated, but also because she hadn't gotten the parting shot.

"You go do yourself, you—you prick," she muttered, stomping into the living room. She seldom used words like that, and found there was a lot of relief in them.

She threw herself down on the couch. How would she ever face him at work again? It was so humiliating. And she would have to see him. Tomorrow. She violently threw all the pillows off the couch, then lay down and wept angrily, venting the tension she was feeling.

After a few minutes she got up and turned on the televison. "I hope he's wandering around out there, lost," she mumbled.

19

Lora dreamed that night about the strange phone call. She was in the same room with the caller and the abusive man—not 1500 miles away, protected from the beating that was going on. Still, she couldn't do anything to help; it was as if her feet were extremely heavy, her legs elephantine. The faceless man stood over the woman kicking her, chanting, "Bitch, bitch, bitch."

No, that wasn't quite it. It was "slitch," a cutting, harsh word which sliced right through you when you heard it. The woman cowered, murmuring, "Hit me, hit me," until she dissolved into a heap of old clothes. Or maybe there had never been a human form there. Maybe the whole dream had been centered around just a pile of trash on the floor. The man turned to Lora and seemed to know she wanted him. Nothing was said in the dream, but the feeling was there, and he came to her and he was on her and her legs were wrapped around him and her body made an orgasmic shudder, awakening her.

They were so vague, dreams were; the details became lost almost as they happened, but their essence remained. And she was disgusted with what the essence seemed to say about her: that she was incapable of doing anything about the man's violence, and that in some way it was even attractive to her. There was that element of desire for him that bothered her. It seemed so masochistic. She didn't like to think of herself like that.

The dream had left her physically relieved, but it was hard to shake off the bad feelings, so she switched on the bedside light and tried to read, but instead began to think about Brad again. Why had she invited him in? She cringed at the memory of the evening. Why had she even gone out with him? She didn't just want to be another person on someone's list. She had led him on, then had acted as if she didn't understand where the evening was supposed to lead. Talk about games. She felt young and naive and incredibly divided within herself. What did she want?

Finally she drifted off to sleep, the paperback lying face down, open on her chest, and the light still burning beside her.

20

Lora felt awful when the alarm went off. She hit the button to silence the dreadful noise, then got up and shuffled, eyes half shut, into the bathroom and plugged in the hot curlers. Her routine was shortened because she had showered the night before, trying to wash away the disgusting evening with Brad, so she headed back to her bedroom to dress, while the rollers heated.

After she had put her makeup on and had done her hair, she grabbed a granola bar on the way out and munched it in the car en route to the office. Her mornings were down to a science, requiring the least amount of time and effort to put on an acceptable appearance. She was not particularly vain, although it did seem that her vanity was increasing in direct proportion to the tiny wrinkles appearing around her eyes. A perversity of nature.

She dreaded seeing Brad—that was the worst thing about today. And he seemed to be flaunting himself in front of her, showing up in Claims frequently, on any pretext. There was no way that his business required so much activity in the Claims Department—always bending over some other rep, talking in his intimate fashion.

He's hoping to make me remorseful over what I missed, she thought. I'll show him he isn't so important. The bastard. She was shocked by her own expletive.

L.J., the California rep, managed to come by her desk once during the morning and said softly, "Something going on between you and lover boy?"

"No way," Lora retorted.

"I thought the way he was panting after you yesterday—"

"Nothing," Lora said, then held up her finger to indicate she had a call. L.J. waved cheerfully and moved away from the desk.

She met her friend Sue for a morning coffee break. One look at Lora and Sue remarked, "I take it your idyllic evening wasn't heaven on earth?"

Lora made a face. "We had a couple of drinks, then a pleasant dinner."

''And . . . ?''

Lora shook her head slowly. ''I invited him to my place for a nightcap and it was a complete fizzle. My fault,'' she said as she put a quarter in the coffee machine and pressed the button, ''completely my fault. I could have hopped in the sack with the dear boy, but no, not me. My virtue, such as it is, remains intact. Oh, shoot, I pressed sugar instead of cream!''

''Hey, relax, Lora,'' Sue said as she got her coffee.

The two of them went to a table and sat down. ''Sue, did you know that upon divorce, maidenly virtue reasserts itself?'' Lora stared down at her cup. ''Am I too nice?''

''Nice?'' Sue snorted. ''I don't exactly see you as nice. I mean, you're not *not* nice, but nice is so blah.''

''That's just my point. I am blah. Look at you. Even the clothes you wear have style, your own style.''

Sue looked down at the dirndl skirt and peasant blouse she was wearing. ''No, let's not look at my clothes,'' she said grinning.

''No, really. I am Miss Everywoman,'' Lora continued. ''Miss Polyester Pants Suit.''

''That's a bit exaggerated. I've never seen you in a polyester pants suit.''

''I might as well be, as exciting as I am. My whole life is in this rut, then I get a chance to liven it up with a man and I blow it.''

''Liven it up with Brad? He's about as exciting as chiggers in East Texas in the summertime. Talk about blah. He is polyester personified. If you want to lose your, uh, virtue, you can do better than Brad.''

''Where? Do you see any decent single men around here?'' She waved her hand to indicate the entire scope of the company.

"Well, give yourself time."

"That's easy for you to say. You've got Kevin, and also you're only thirty-two."

"So, you're ancient? Lora, Brad is a . . . a nerd."

Sue's derision made Lora feel a little better, and nerd, as a description of Brad, made her giggle.

"But Sue, it was awful."

"Don't worry about it. He's just not the right person for you. And you're not blah. You're a warm, caring person."

"You make me feel better," Lora said, but she sighed, and Sue raised her eyebrows. "I just need to make some changes in my life, Sue. It's stagnant. I can't take many more of these evenings, cuddled up—with my TV set."

"You'll have to come over some evening and have dinner with us."

Lora thanked her, but knew that wouldn't do it. She wanted a man in her life. And yet she could see the fallacy in being as dependent as she had been. Look what it had gotten her. First a divorce, then sort of a chronic diminishment of self-esteem.

They talked about how obviously Brad was showing up in Claims today, and laughed a bit about it, which lifted Lora's mood considerably. She took the last drink in her cup, making another face. "That's terrible stuff," she said.

But Sue didn't hear her; she was gazing over Lora's shoulder. "There goes Mr. Wonderful himself. He's with his next conquest, no doubt."

Lora felt the color rising in her face. Conquest. Well, she hadn't been that exactly.

"Look cool," Sue advised. "He's nothing. Not worthy of your attention."

Lora smiled at her. "Thanks, Sue." She reached over and patted her hand. "We'd better be getting back."

"Hey, did the cops get hold of you?" Sue asked on the way back to their section.

"No. Did they call for me?"

"Yeah. Yesterday just as you left. Something about that woman you overheard."

"Oh, I thought you meant the local police. I knew I'd get a call if I left early."

"I gave him your home phone; hope that was okay."

Lora nodded. "Sure. But he must have called while I was out with Brad."

Back at her desk there was a note for her to stop by Marge's desk in personnel. So before she settled in again, she took the elevator down to the first floor, then wound her way through the maze of the building till she came to the right office. She pulled the door open with such force that she took it out of a man's hand who was coming out. She noticed he was slim and quite handsome, before averting her eyes. "Sorry," she said with a laugh, "I guess I don't know my own strength."

He didn't return her friendliness, but eyed her coldly while stepping back for her to pass into the office before he left.

"If looks could kill," she said to herself as she went into Marge's cubicle.

"What are you muttering about?" Marge asked.

"Oh, nothing. I got your note."

"You said you wanted to adjust your withholding, so I need you to fill this out." She shoved a form at Lora, who sat down and began to read it, but before she got far, Brad came out of his cubicle. "Marge—" he started, then stopped. "Oh. You're busy." He narrowed his eyes at Lora.

Another dirty look, Lora thought. I'm batting a thousand.

"Lora's just filling out a W-4 for me. What do you need?"

"Did I set my staff directory down in here?"

Marge rummaged around in the stuff on her desk. "Don't see it."

He shrugged and went back into his own area, out of sight.

Well, thought Lora, perhaps dirty looks will be the worst of it and things with Brad could get back to—well, if not the way they used to be, at least back to neutral.

21

Bill Graham flopped down in his favorite easy chair, located the television's remote control device among the papers on a footstool, then pressed the channel select. But he wasn't really watching the parade of images in front of him.

It had been a rough day. A mentally-deranged father had been holed up in an apartment building, with his ex-wife and three children as hostages. Bill had been there since early that morning, trying to talk the guy into coming out or, at least, into sending the others out. Mainly, of course, he had been waiting.

The trouble came because the man's ex-wife had let some other guy move into *his* apartment—that's what the perpetrator called it, *his* apartment. He paid his child support nice and regular like and he didn't want to be supporting a place for "no S.O.B." drunk to live.

His concern for his children didn't seem to be the real issue, since he was armed heavily and was threatening to blow the apartment building to smithereens, nor did the apartment he was paying rent on seem to matter. It was simply a statement he was making about the whole system of broken homes, no-good ex-wives, child support, and, of course, drunken boyfriends.

The apartment had been evacuated. Trying to get people up and out had been a task, something you wouldn't expect. There was a certain resistance to leaving the protection of one's place, even when it no longer was safe. It reminded him of the people who froze to death in their own homes rather than go to a heated public building. One old man had temporarily barricaded himself into his own apartment in sympathy, saying he understood and agreed. The whole world was wacko.

He hated waiting. He had had his share of it when he was in the Army. Intelligence, they called it. What it had meant was he spent a lot of time waiting outside of bars on stakeouts. God, it was boring. Somehow the name "Intelligence" conjured up spies. But he never was involved in anything with any security risk, all just rinky-dink stuff, guys ripping off merchandise at the commissary, AWOLs, guys selling dope, things like that.

He had been stationed at Fort Bliss when he was in "Intelligence." He and Marianne and their son Patrick had lived in a little two-bedroom house on the base. Despite the boring nature of the work, those had been a couple of good years. Marianne had been happy in El Paso. And so he had been happy, too.

He remembered, fondly, trips over the border, when they drank tequila in cheap bars, wandered through the

Mexican market, buying trinkets to send back to relatives on the east coast who had never been west of the Mississippi.

God, that was a long time ago, he thought. I was only twenty-three then. Imagine, a twenty-three-year-old on a stakeout. Talk about green behind the ears. He hadn't even had his full growth. But he hadn't felt that way then. He had felt like Mr. Big.

He was musing about the old days when another officer approached him. "Just got word, Lieutenant. The guy wants to talk."

Ah, a break, he thought. The first chink. Maybe we'll get this wrapped up before evening.

And they had. But the waiting had taken its toll, and he was bone weary by the time he got home. An evening of mindless channel switching seemed to be the balm he needed, till he fell asleep in his chair. Then he remembered that he needed to call Lora Montgomery. Or was the operative word "wanted" instead of "needed"? No matter, he felt miraculously alert as he went to the phone.

22

She dashed into her place after work, changed into her jeans and a T-shirt, ran a brush through her hair, and put on some lipstick. It took less than five minutes, then she grabbed her purse and went back to the car.

The traffic was tedious, and what should have been a

three-minute drive took about ten. She pulled in at Angelo's, a singles bar, went in, looked around and realized she was one of the few there. Wednesday. Not a big happy-hour day.

She sat down at the bar and the bartender said, "Hiya, kiddo. What can I do you?"

"A draft," she replied. The door opened, letting in the bright outside light. She turned to see who was coming in, if there was any hope. She could just see the outline of a man. She swiveled her stool back to the bar as the beer was served.

The newcomer came over to the bar and sat down one stool away from her. He ordered a beer. She could feel the silent appraisal going on, so she looked over at him to make eye contact.

She smiled slightly, brushed her hair away from her face, and said, "Getting your eyes full?"

He just looked at her, a half smile on his face to match hers.

"Here you are, buddy," the bartender said as he sat the beer down. "We'll have some hors d'oeuvres out in a minute."

"Thanks."

Several more men came in, and she looked, but no one was as interesting looking as the first. They didn't say anything for a while, but when she had almost finished her first beer, he said, "May I buy you another?"

"Why not?"

He raised two fingers to the bartender, who was down the bar, and indicated their almost-empty glasses. When they were served, the man moved over next to her.

"I hear they have these fantastic fried mushrooms here," she told him as the food was being put out.

"I'd like to try a fried mushroom." They went to the spread of food and filled plates, then went to a table instead of back to the bar.

"Do you work around here?"

"I'm in real estate," he told her.

That sounded good, although the way the economy was, maybe not so good as a year or so earlier.

"What about you?" he asked.

"United Assurance. Claims rep."

"The big office building down the way?" he asked, indicating the direction.

"Uh-huh," she said, biting the cap off a mushroom and rolling it around in her mouth. She licked the edge of her mouth tantalizingly, slowly, with the tip of her tongue, while she fixed his gaze.

"Pretty interesting work?"

She shrugged. "We get our share of weirdos. There was one yesterday. A woman got beat up."

"What d'ya mean?"

"Well, it was just a case of overhearing this—this assault." She ran her hand through her hair, leaned back and closed her eyes. After a moment she reopened them lazily and leaned toward him, both elbows on the table, then in a soft voice asked, "Did you ever hear the word 'slitch'?"

He shook his head.

"Neither had I. That's what he called her." She enunciated it slowly, directed toward him, "A slitch." Then she shuddered. "I need another round. How about you?"

He ordered, then asked her, "What do you do in a case like that? Report it?"

She looked at him, puzzled.

"You know, the assault you heard."

"Oh, well, it's no job for a claims representative." The waiter came with their beers, then she asked her companion his name. "I wouldn't want to ask a stranger over for pizza."

"Do you have that in mind?"

"If he'll come," she said, propping herself up with one elbow, her wrist under her chin. "I have one in the freezer."

"Sounds just like home," he commented.

"*Mi casa es su casa,*" she said, her voice slurring as she leaned toward him and put her manicured nail against his lips. He opened his mouth slightly and took hold of her fingernail with his teeth.

"Let's get out of here," he said.

Just as they got to the door, it opened. Brad Conroy and a dark-haired woman she didn't know came in. "Imagine meeting you here," Brad said.

She murmured a hello to him, then giggled, too giddy to be conversational. Brad turned to her companion and said, "Hello, again. Brad Conroy." He shoved his hand out.

She struggled with the heavy door, then felt it effortlessly open. She liked a man who took control.

"I'd better drive," he suggested as they got outside. "Which one is your car?"

She pointed it out, then he led her to it and helped her.

"Do you think I had one too many?"

"Maybe. Too much before dinner. It'll wear off by the time we have pizza. Just tell me where you live."

She did, then leaned back against the seat, closing her eyes. Things seemed to spin, but it was okay; it would wear off soon enough. She was enjoying the sensation.

At her place he unlocked the door, but she was navigating better. "Make yourself at home while I go to the little girl's room," she said. She relieved herself for what seemed forever, then kicked off her shoes and went back into the living room. He was just putting a record on the stereo. As it began to play she swaggered up to him seductively, putting her smooth arms around his neck. "Want to dance?" she asked.

He put his arms around her waist and pulled her to him, holding her tighter and tighter. At first she was enjoying it—what seemed to be the insistence of his need—but then it went too far.

"Hey, you're hurting me," she said thickly.

"Have you reported that phone call to the police?"

"What are you talking about? Let me go!" The stereo seemed louder than before to her. Things were taking on a nightmarish quality.

"You know what I'm talking about. The woman you heard being beat up. The hit-and-run. Did you call the fucking cops?" He spat the words out, bending her farther and farther back, until she fell down on the couch.

"I didn't call the cops, you bastard. It wasn't my call. It was Lora Montgomery's, so how the hell should I know if she called the cops? Now let me go." She was still confident that she could handle the situation. This guy was some kind of a nut, but she had handled lots of weirdos in the past. But why did this one have to turn out weird? He was so good-looking.

Her last remarks startled him, and he relaxed his grip for a moment. She slithered sideways on the couch, away from him, but he was back on her in an instant. "You slitch," he muttered as his hand closed on her neck. "You're nothing but a cheap whore."

That word again. Slitch.

23

Lora got out of her car and went to the mailbox at the curb. There were several pieces of junk mail and a photocopied flyer someone had stuck in the box without postage, announcing a meeting on Friday evening to organize a neighborhood watch program.

She didn't much want to go to a neighborhood meeting, but the idea of a neighborhood watch sounded like a good one. She wasn't often scared, but occasionally she would hear something in the middle of the night that would frighten her; if signs scattered around saying the neighbors were alert would act as a deterrent, a watch couldn't hurt.

Jack Turner pulled up across the street just then, hopped out of his car and walked over. "Hi, hon." Their relationship had remained neighborly over the months. They often talked when one or the other was in the yard, but she had never again asked him in.

"Hello, Jack," she replied.

"I've got an extra beer over there, just waiting to be drunk. Want to come over?"

She smiled. "No, I've got plans," she lied. "But thanks."

"Lucky you. I'll be sitting over there, bored, and you'll be out painting the town."

She raised her eyebrows. "Ah-hah, jumping to conclusions,'' she chided him. ''Did I say I had a date?'' She handed him her copy of the flyer, saying, ''Here's something to think about while you're bored.''

He looked it over. ''Hmmm. Pretty good idea. Guess I will have something to think about. These bozos out here may need my advice. You going? I could take you over.''

''No, I won't be there,'' she said, deciding right then. ''But tell them I'm in favor of it.''

''Sure will, little lady. I agree with you. Never hurts to keep an eye on one another. Right?'' He raised his eyebrows.

''I guess not. Well, I have to be getting in now. Let me know what happens.''

''Sure thing.''

She escaped into the house, kicking off her shoes by the front door. As she tore open the mail, she wondered where all the trees were coming from to support the flood of paper that filled mailboxes daily. Today alone there was an invitation to a time-share resort, a burial-policy plan, and, ironically, an invitation to contribute to a nationwide conservation organization. She shook her head, then carefully opened the only quality mail in the lot, a letter from her mother. It was a connection she cherished but hadn't done much to nurture since the divorce. What could she write to her parents? There was not much happening in her life. Dear Mother, I answered twenty-three claims calls today. Love, Lora. She didn't want to mention Martin because they would get their hopes up that somehow the rift in the ''family'' would right itself. Martin had been a much-loved son-in-law, the son her father had never had. Now he didn't seem to have a position in the family. If there had been children and he'd been the custodial parent—which was unlikely—then they probably would have maintained a close connection, even at her emotional expense.

Sometimes she wanted to write home and say how confused she was, but what would that help? It would just be an exercise in self-indulgence.

Her mother's letter was full of news about Lora's happily married sister in Abilene, what the grandkids were doing, all about Uncle George's triple-bypass surgery and whether it was really necessary, and Dad putting out the tomato sets. Lora sighed, refolded the letter, and slid it back into its envelope. She stuck it in a kitchen drawer and dropped the other mail in the trash can in the kitchen before heading down the hall to her bedroom.

She pulled her skirt off, then began to pull her blouse over her head. She had forgotten to undo the one button at the back of the neckline, and felt a momentary sense of panic when she got it up around her head and couldn't get it off. She fought to get it back down and off her face, and succeeding, took a deep breath to calm her unreasonable panic, undid the button and started over. As a child she had suffered from allergies, had been a mouth breather till she was an adolescent. Once when she and her sister were really young, they decided to get wrapped up like mummies. They rummaged in the rag bag for cloth to make into wrappings, then thought of the adhesive tape, in the medicine cabinet. They started on Lora, who was smaller. Her sister thought Lora was doing a pretty good acting job as the mummy when she began to claw at the tape, with her already wrapped hands, to get it off her mouth so she could breathe. They didn't play Mummy again.

Now, there were occasionally situations that reminded her of that awful feeling, and she generally avoided them. Maybe it accounted for her love of the outdoors. Not that she was a sportsperson, but a warm spring day like this one could work its magic on her, revitalizing her, making her eager to get out into the yard to plant something. She had ordered some seeds during an ice storm in the dead of winter, a pleasant way to remind herself that there really would be a spring again.

She slipped into her blue jeans and a T-shirt she had bought one day when she went to the zoo with Martin before the divorce. It, too, had been a pleasant spring day, and they had been contented and happy. At least she had thought so. It was odd how the divorce had somehow contaminated all the memories of the times before.

All the talk about growing apart, she thought, is flawed. We didn't grow apart; we fell apart in the space of three months. She could look back and recall little hints that he was suddenly dissatisfied; for instance, when he lost interest in things he had routinely done for years—like yard work—and suddenly developed an interest in other things, like being a snappy dresser. Designer clothes on Martin? That had been a real switch, but one she hadn't recognized as a red flag until much later. It was the same time that "the other woman" had started working closely with Martin. She was having marital troubles, and he listened to her, something her husband had never done. Lora always thought of that with chagrin because she could remember complaining to Martin about his reading at the table, when they could be talking.

Lora realized she was thinking herself into the blues, so she forced herself to switch mental gears as she rummaged around in the junk drawer in the kitchen and found the seed packages buried near the bottom, underneath cords, clothespins, and light bulbs. Bachelor buttons, anemones, petunias—she had forgotten what she had ordered. She read the backs of the packages to see if it was too early to plant them, then went into the garage to find some gardening tools.

When she had gotten her hands into the warm earth in the backyard and planted the seeds, she faintly heard the phone ring. At first she thought it must be the neighbors', but then realized it was hers. Should I struggle to get it? she asked herself. No, I probably won't make it.

The ringing was persistent, though, so she finally changed her mind, rubbed her hands off on the grass as a temporary measure, stood up and hurried into the house. By the time she answered, there was just a dial tone. Surely whoever it was would try again if it were important.

She had just gotten back into the yard and down on her knees when the phone rang again. She rolled her eyes, sighed, and this time practically broke her neck getting inside in a hurry.

"Hello?" If this is Martin, she thought, I'll croak.

"Ms. Andrews?"

"Yes?"

It was the police lieutenant, Bill Graham, from New York. "I wanted to touch base with you," he said, "because of what's happened here." He hesitated a moment, then continued. "We were investigating a hit-and-run, you know that, and we had a woman come in and report that her car was missing. It matched the description of the vehicle involved in the hit-and-run. To make a long story short, we went over to the woman's house after your call, and we found her dead. She'd been beaten up. I feel sure that she's the woman you heard on the phone. Her name was Shera Johnson."

Lora drew her breath in audibly. "It was that poor little timid woman I talked to on Monday. I'm sure that was her name. She called me about her missing car and I told her she had to report it to the police."

"She did that, and we told her that a car matching her car's description had been involved in this hit-and-run. It was the next morning that she called you—I guess that was the second time she had talked to you, right?"

"Yes."

"And you overheard her murder."

"Do you know who killed her?"

"Her landlady said her boyfriend was there that morning. It looks as if he was involved in the hit-and-run—just from a physical description a witness gave us."

"And that's why, when he heard her calling me about a hit-and-run, he became so violent."

"Probably."

"Probably?"

"Nothing's certain. We haven't picked him up yet—can't find him."

"I appreciate your telling me about what happened. I don't usually associate this kind of, well, follow-up with the police."

He gave a brief laugh.

"Did I say something funny?"

"No, not at all. That was a self-conscious laugh, I guess, because I'm off duty."

"Oh." She didn't know quite what to say next, and apparently neither did he, because there was a noticeable silence.

"Well, I do appreciate it," Lora finally said, kicking herself for not being more chatty, so that she could find out what had motivated him to call her. "Thank you."

"You're welcome," he said. "I guess that's all for now. I'll let you know if there are any other developments."

She smiled as she put the phone back on its cradle, keeping her hand on it momentarily to keep the connection, sensing something more in the call, in the nuance in his voice. He's in New York, you idiot, she reminded herself.

Her smiled vanished when she remembered the message he had delivered. That woman—dead. It was awful. Lora went back outside, but somehow the day was not as sunshiny as before. It was flawed by a faraway violence which had touched her world through the telephone.

24

The wrong person. How could he be such a screw-up? He had killed the wrong person.

Earlier, he'd combed the United Assurance staff directory looking for the name Laura and had been lucky enough to find only one—Laura Andrews—in the claims section. Then he'd wasted an hour sitting outside her address, waiting for her to appear. And just as he'd thought about getting out of the car to go up to the apartment, she had come out again. Everything had worked out fine; she hadn't met anyone else at the bar. She was just a pickup, waiting for him. Then to find out she wasn't the right person—*Christ Almighty*.

When she had said, "Not me," he had felt the excitement of his impending violence dwindle. But he had to go on and kill her. He had had no choice. He couldn't explain away his actions. And he still didn't know if the police were on to him. He briefly wondered if Shera's body had been found, wondered if he should call his mother to find out if she knew anything. He quickly put the thought aside, knowing it would be suicide. The police, if they were on to him, would be listening in. The toughest thing was not knowing what was happening back there.

He drew both hands up across his temples and through his hair, shaking his head. That music. Rap. So loud. He had to get it turned off; it aggravated the shock he was feeling.

He turned the stereo off, letting the needle remain on the record as it came to a stop, then went to the kitchen and got a towel off the handle of the refrigerator. Back in the living room he carefully wiped down the stereo and the record he had touched, then looked around to see if there was anything else, but he really hadn't been there long enough to leave many prints.

He left the woman draped across the couch. A random victim, a motiveless murder, for all the world would know. That's what it would look like. Then he remembered that guy—what the hell was his name anyway? Brad Conley, something like that. He could link him to Laura tonight. But it would take a while for someone to find the body—she had told him she didn't have a roommate—then, when they found the body, it would take a while to make the connection.

Do I need to kill the guy? The muscle at the corner of Tony's mouth tightened, stretching his lower lip into a one-sided grimace. *He doesn't know anything about me, not one damn thing, except how I look, and by the time they get it all figured out, I can be on my way back home, all the strings tied.*

Convincing himself that he was safe for at least another twenty-four hours, he dropped any notion of tracking Brad down. He just needed to get on with what he came here to do. That was enough to occupy him for now.

He opened the door and peered out cautiously, to make sure no one was looking, then went to her car and got in. He carefully wiped the steering wheel and the door handles. Once he was satisfied that the car, too, was clean, he got out, leaving the towel on the seat, and jogged the few blocks back to the bar, where he had left Bart's car.

He started the car and headed back toward Bart's. He guessed he wouldn't be able to put off getting the Dallas tour this evening. He had pleaded business today, and Bart, who it turned out was on vacation till Friday evening, insisted he take the car—hoping to make him feel more indebted, Tony thought.

Tony leaned on his horn when a driver in front of him didn't take off as soon as the light changed from red to green. Once the guy started, Tony goosed the accelerator and shot expertly around him. But his mind wasn't on his driving. He was thinking about how complicated things were getting. By tomorrow at the earliest, they'd find Laura Andrews and would be looking for someone here. If he were lucky, he'd have longer than that. But it was essential to kill Lora tomorrow.

He whipped onto Bart's street, searching for the right house. Finally he wheeled into the driveway, thinking how the place looked kind of like a sanctuary, with the lamplight welcoming him through the window shades. He noticed that Lonnie's car was there.

"Hey, you're home," Bart said as Tony came in. "You just got here in time. I made that chili I promised you." The thought almost turned Tony's stomach after the beer and greasy mushrooms, but when Bart called him and Lonnie to the table, he went.

He took a bite and felt the flame rise in his throat. "Goddamn," he railed. He grabbed his water glass and gulped some down.

Lonnie and Bart started laughing.

"That's the hottest damn stuff I've ever eaten," he said, still gasping. Lonnie and Bart were just sitting there smiling, shoveling the stuff in like cucumber soup.

"Told you it would blow your socks off."

25

Martin, Lora's ex-husband, left his girlfriend Serena's apartment without reluctance. She had three children under ten, the four of them crammed into a two-bedroom apartment, and the ambience was anything but tranquil. They needed a bigger place, something with a yard, but they hadn't found anything suitable they could afford on Serena's salary, and Leon, her ex, was out of work at the moment, so he was no help. Now he was on his way over to take the oldest boy to a Little League game. Martin didn't particularly want to run into him. Ruefully, he remembered his first meeting with Leon.

There had come this thunderous knock on the door, and Serena, in bed with Martin, had whispered that they should ignore it. But it became hard to ignore, particularly when the door began to rattle and a loud voice shouted, "God-damn it, Rena, I know you're in there, so open the door."

Martin had felt trapped like a rat in a bucket filling with water. He jumped up and jerked his pants on, not wanting to get caught in such a vulnerable state of undress. Meanwhile, Serena grabbed a robe and went to answer the door, warning Martin to stay put in the bedroom. In fact, she went even further, saying, "He has an awful temper when he's been drinking."

"Has he been?" Martin asked.

"What?" Serena asked, preoccupied with what seemed like fear to Martin.

"Drinking. Has he been drinking?"

She nodded. "Maybe you'd better get in the closet."

"You must be kidding."

"He's mean, Martin, and big." She convinced him.

How do grown-up people get involved in such things? he wondered from his position in the closet, where he could hear Leon ranting at Serena. God, why didn't Leon stop and go home? Serena certainly wasn't encouraging him to stay. She kept telling him she wanted to be alone, but Leon wouldn't listen. That was the trouble with drunks, Martin thought, they get diarrhea of the mouth.

"How 'bout we go do it, Rena? C'mon, baby. I could use a little lovin'." He went on and on.

Martin wanted to throw up, listening to this guy. What a clown. Lord, I hope she doesn't agree, he thought. He couldn't imagine having to listen to them thumping around on the bed.

After squatting for a good half hour, both his legs were asleep and Leon hadn't gotten any nearer the bedroom, so Martin decided to stretch. He tried to stand up, but the sleeping legs wouldn't cooperate; he tumbled out of the closet, which was something of a disaster area, it was so overloaded with Serena's things.

Of course, Leon heard him. Martin had recovered enough by the time Leon got into the bedroom to be standing, at least, and he was sure glad he had his pants on. This was his first sight of Leon, and he was proud that he didn't quake in his bare feet. This guy looked like a fullback for the pros. While Martin was muscular, he suddenly felt like Mickey Mouse before this towering monstrosity. What was really disgusting was the head of hair the guy had. It grew like a rug. Martin reached up self-consciously to the balding spot on the back of his head and rubbed it, while he felt color rising up into his very high—and growing higher every year—forehead. "Hi," he said, in some kind of an understatement for the occasion. "I'm a friend of Serena's."

Leon was too surprised to say much of anything. His jaw dropped open, and Serena was good enough to take up the slack in conversation by ordering him out of the apartment. She made it good by adding, "Once and for all." Miraculously for Martin, Leon complied, muttering obscenities on the way out. Martin left shortly afterward, too, the moment being somehow ruined.

The "once and for all" was just temporary. Leon came by to see the kids a couple of times each week, and Martin tried not to be there.

He decided he would just drive back to Dallas and drop in on Lora—see what she was up to tonight. Better than returning to his lonely apartment.

26

Just as Lora was putting up her gardening tools, she heard the familiar sound of Martin's car pulling up in the driveway. She went back into the house through the garage and got to the front door just as he approached it.

"Hi, Lora," he said, with a look on his face she didn't trust.

"Hello, Martin," she replied in a resigned tone.

"Tried to get hold of you last evening. Did you have a date?"

She flared. "Martin, I do have a private life now, you know. You're not my keeper." She moved inside, and he followed her.

"I never was your keeper. May I sit down?" he asked, rhetorically, as he flopped on the couch.

"Well, maybe you should have been a little more so. Maybe that was what was wrong." Yes, she thought to herself, maybe that was it. "You never expected one thing of me, not one blasted thing, and then if I expected anything from you, you were quick to point out that you didn't make demands on me, so why did I make demands on you? I've thought a lot about it, and I think there have to be some expectations on both sides of a marriage. The way it was, you came off as giving everything and taking nothing. And I always ended up feeling selfish and that you were right and I was bad.''

''Hell, Lora, don't start something,'' he said, rejecting any serious discussion about their marriage.

She sighed—here she was, being bad again, trying to start something, according to him. But she retorted, ''Me? I didn't start anything. You come dropping in here unannounced, wanting to know where I was last night, and then tell me I'm starting something.'' She got up huffily and went into the kitchen to get herself a glass of tea. ''You want some tea?'' she yelled at him.

''No. I'm not staying.''

She went back into the living room, and he was already standing up to go, looking much younger than his forty years, in his T-shirt and jeans and Nikes. ''Why *did* you come by?'' she asked acerbically.

He shrugged and boyishly said, ''Didn't have anything to do this evening. But I can see you don't want my company.''

She sighed, closed her eyes momentarily, then opened them and said, ''I'm sorry, Martin, I didn't mean to get angry. But you don't have any right to ask me what I was doing last night. Not anymore.''

''I know,'' he said sheepishly. ''Sorry.''

''Did you just get off work? Or did you drive clear back over here from home?''

''I went home first.''

''Well, then, you'd better stay awhile. To make it worth the trip.'' He and Serena both lived in a suburb halfway between Dallas and Fort Worth, but worked in Dallas. They had met at the Laundromat. ''Unless you have plans with Serena.''

''No.'' He grinned. ''Leon was coming by to take Jason

to a Little League game." He had shared the story of Leon with Lora shortly after it happened. That was one thing Lora appreciated about Martin: he could laugh at himself.

"I can grill some hamburgers," she said. "I thawed some ground beef today." She frowned. "May have to eat the hamburgers on bread. I don't think I have any buns."

He gave her a lascivious grin and said, "I won't say the obvious—bread will be okay."

She couldn't help but smile at him. She still felt susceptible to his heavy-duty build, the straw-colored close-cropped hair, which had begun to recede in Martin's twenties, the pale blue eyes with flecks of green. Martin looked so dependable and . . . nice, which wasn't titillating, but comfortable.

"Come on outside with me and I'll show you what I've been doing in the garden. And maybe you'll start some charcoal." Like a hundred other evenings, she thought.

She made an effort during the evening not to bring up the past, to keep things on a friendly level. They watched some television, then Martin, pleading the long drive home, got up to leave when the news came on.

After he left, Lora made sure all the doors and windows were locked. As she walked through the house, it suddenly seemed awfully quiet. She pulled her jeans and T-shirt off, stuffed them in the washer, then went down the hall to the bedroom and took a nightgown from her drawer. After a quick shower she slipped into the gown, got into bed and lay there awhile, but her mind was racing—a hodgepodge of disquieting thoughts about that poor woman and Bill Graham and Martin. She couldn't get comfortable. A neighbor dog began to bark, then another and another, until their voices echoed loneliness for blocks around.

Finally she turned on the bedside lamp, got up, and

raised the bedroom window just a little, adjusting the blind. She felt uneasy opening it, but maybe a little fresh air would help her drift off to sleep. She hurriedly got back in bed and punched the pillow behind her several times to fluff it up, then took the novel she was reading from the nightstand, glad it was a romance and not a thriller.

A noise from the other room startled her, just a settling house sound, and she burrowed farther under the covers as a shiver went up her spine.

27

He found it an auspicious sign when he saw her lights go back on. The gods smile on those who wait, he thought ruefully.

He approached the lighted window behind the shrubs cautiously, and his caution served him well, because just then she opened the window. He pulled back momentarily, but he could still see the delicious shape of her body through the sheer, cotton-candy-colored nightgown. She was so close, and the night so quiet, that he could hear her sigh as she picked up a paperback book from the nightstand beside the bed. He almost felt he was in the room with her, that he could speak and she wouldn't be startled. But, of course, he knew that was foolish.

She looked extremely attractive there with her hair tousled, the ends of it in wet tendrils from the shower, her face shiny clean. He could only see the bodice of her nightgown, her nipples temptingly exposed through the semi-opaque nylon. She looked very feminine and very vulnerable, especially against the pale blue of the sheets and blanket. Baby colors. He noticed her shudder, then scoot farther under the covers. It brought a responsive shudder from him.

He must be careful. The thought brought a frown to his face. He suppressed a sigh which she might have heard, then reached down and unzipped his pants.

28

Serena answered the door after the third knock—not long, considering the time of night. "Hi," she said wearily.

"Hi. Can I come in?" Martin asked.

"Isn't everything all right at Lora's?"

He frowned as he came into the room. "What do you mean?"

"You always come running over here after you've been there. It's like you go over there and try to pick up the pieces of your marriage and then, when it doesn't work, run back to me."

It was embarrassing to have his behavior so exposed. Lora would feed him, talk to him, let him fix things around the house, but it wasn't like it used to be. Still, it was hard to stay away. And he always left feeling frustrated by those two facts. So he used Serena.

He had admitted almost from the night he'd asked for it that the divorce was probably a mistake. As he'd said the words, they sounded like a script from a bad movie. But it was hard to stop the forward momentum, and then, later, so many things were said. It was hard to undo those words. Even now they both sometimes lashed out cruelly, bringing up unforgiven sins from years ago.

What Lora had said this evening, though, felt right. She'd hit on something. He remembered once when she had asked him to help her make up the bed and he'd replied that he didn't care if the bed was made, so why should he spend his time making it. And then he'd lapsed into his song and dance about not expecting things of her, that he accepted her as she was and didn't expect her to do what she didn't want to. It was a little embarrassing to realize he had said it so often that she could quote him. Not that the bedmaking was a big event, but it represented what she was talking about. He remembered that particular incident because they had argued and she'd called him self-righteous. As he stood there, he could feel she was indeed correct—he did feel self-righteous—but it made him even more determined to prove his point. She had ended up crying and feeling contrite and he remembered her telling him, "I know what you're saying is logical and it's the way it ought to be, but then why do I feel so bad?" If he was right, then why had he felt so bad, too? Why did they both end up losing?

For a couple of months he'd thought there was a possibility they might get back together, if he'd just hang around. That would please both their families. He realized Lora was still testing the waters, unable or unwilling to forgive and forget. Maybe with time . . .

But now, for him, there had been time enough. He was

lonely; he was tired of the potential cafeteria of women, because the cafeteria usually turned out to have only appetizers, with no main courses or desserts. Marriage was more like the main course, with occasional desserts. Oddly enough, he guessed he wanted to go back into a situation where there was something expected of him. Expectations.

"Sorry," he murmured now to Serena. "I didn't know it bothered you."

She shrugged. "I guess it doesn't too much or I wouldn't let you in. Want some coffee?"

"No. Can I—may I stay over?"

She gave a little snort of a laugh. "Why not? Good ol' Serena."

"Hey, I won't if—"

"It's okay. In fact, I'd like you to. I'm just feeling kind of cynical. Leon stopped in when he brought Jason home."

"Oh. What did he want?"

"I guess it's sort of like when you go by Lora's. He's just testing."

"Had he been drinking?"

"No. He's been sober every time I've seen him lately."

"Has he been wanting you to come back?"

"I kind of get that feeling."

Martin thought about that a moment, wondering what kind of impact it would have on his life.

"Would you consider it?"

"I'm awfully tired."

Martin thought she meant she wanted to go to bed, but before he suggested they turn in, she continued.

"Living alone with the kids is really difficult—getting them ready for school, being the only one to do everything. It's amazing that even as little help as Leon was, he was there. Like when they were sick. Somehow he could share the . . . scary part of it."

"Serena?"

"Yeah?"

"I don't mean to—to use you."

"Don't worry about it. I've always been everybody's friend. You know?"

He went over to her and put his arms around her. "You're more than that."

"Am I?"

They made love. It was quick and efficient, only flawed when Martin murmured "Lora" instead of "Serena" into Serena's ear. She was patient about it, only stiffening slightly. Funny, she never called him Leon. It was ironic, since Lora often got mad at him because he would slip and call her Serena.

After Serena was sleeping quietly by his side, he began to think about what he'd meant when he said she was more than a friend. He did care about her. Serena was always there when he needed her. And he hoped he was around when she needed him—except when Leon was there, he thought dryly. But if he and Serena were married, they could deal with that. Marriage would give him a legitimate place in her life, and Leon would be just someone from the past. They could make arrangements about the kids.

He hadn't particularly wanted children, although Lora had. His idea was that their life was all right. Why take a chance on screwing up their marriage with kids? It would be strange if he ended up with a family and she didn't. Serve him right, he thought unbidden, then wondered what he really meant. There was still a lot he didn't understand about his and Lora's relationship. He guessed he never would.

He turned his head and looked at Serena, wanting to

reach out and stroke her hair, tears springing into his eyes. She hadn't pushed him about getting married; he appreciated that. But maybe it was time to consider it. Maybe it really was over between him and Lora. Maybe the future was with Serena. He tried to imagine how he would feel if she remarried Leon. Lonely, yes. Resigned. He was feeling resigned a lot lately. He really ought to do something about it.

The digital clock said three A.M., but his eyes just wouldn't close. He just kept staring at the ceiling, wondering why he had ever gotten himself into this lonely scene.

29

At her desk Lora adjusted her headset. "Claims. Lora speaking."

A short pause, then, "Hi, Lora," a male voice said. "I want to report a missing tape deck. Are you the person I report it to?"

"I'm the New York representative, yes."

"You don't sound like a New Yorker," came the voice from the other end of the line.

"You're right." Lora punched a screen on her computer. "I'm in Texas. This is a wide area service line."

"Well, of course, I guess I knew that." The person let out a little laugh. "I like your accent. You have a nice voice."

"Thank you." Lora saw Brad coming toward her desk.

"Texas. Where in Texas?" the voice asked.

"Dallas." Brad came right to her desk and stopped. She tried to focus her attention on her computer screen. "Now about your claim—"

"That's a coincidence."

"What?" Lora asked, confused.

"About your being in Dallas, because I'm flying there on business. I don't suppose—" he broke off.

"What?" She kept her eyes safely down, but her face felt as if it were turning bright red.

"Oh, an idle thought. I'm sure you wouldn't—you're probably happily married with a couple of little ones to go home to."

"No."

"No to the 'married' or just not to the 'happily'?"

"To both, I guess."

"Well, would you . . . would you meet me for a drink, maybe?" His voice had changed from confidence to one of appeal. "I don't know anyone there in Dallas and I'll have some time on my hands. Just a drink. I know you don't know me, but we'd be in a public place."

Lora's eyes, with a will of their own, glanced up at Brad, and their eyes met. He had such a self-satisfied look on his face that she wanted to hit him. What was he hovering around here for anyway?

"Sure, why not," she said decisively into the phone. "When are we talking about?"

"Friday."

"Where will you be staying?"

The man hesitated. "I have to confirm my reservations, so let me call you back later, okay?"

"Sure."

"Well, bye for now, then."

"Wait, I didn't get your name." But he had already hung up.

"Business, I presume?" Brad said cattily.

"None of yours," she said, smiling just as cattily. She straightened up and dropped the lock of hair she had been unconsciously twisting. Things weren't quite neutral yet. "Did you want something?"

"No, just passing by," he said, and with a look of acute disdain, he sauntered away.

Shortly afterward Sue found an excuse to come by her desk. "What was that all about?" she asked.

"Nothing. At least we've spoken, that's about all I can say. Oh, Lord, he's a case. I feel as if I'm back in high school, that's how juvenile he is."

"Maybe you're just on his mind," Sue said.

"I doubt that. I think he just feels like he's making me eat my heart out." She giggled. "And I can hardly stand to think that he thinks I might be."

Her musings over Brad made her forget to mention the blind date until she and Sue went on break.

"You call yourself blah?" Sue asked. "I would never accept a date like that."

"Kevin would hardly like it," Lora said, speaking of the man with whom Sue lived.

"Even if Kevin weren't in the picture."

"I couldn't believe it when I heard myself saying, yes," Lora admitted. "But there was Brad, and," she shrugged, "it just happened. He's probably going to report me for having a personal phone call on company time."

"You be mighty careful, girl," Sue warned. "Remember when L.J. went out with that guy with the foot fetish? Speaking of whom—not him, but her—I wonder where she is today? Too much partying, do you suppose? I'm having to take her calls, which really pisses me off."

"Probably. I wish I could be as casual about my social life as she seems about hers."

"There are too many weirdos around these days for that. Not to mention STDs."

"STDs? What are those?" Lora asked.

"Where have you been? Don't you read the news magazines? Sexually-transmitted diseases—AIDS, stuff like that."

Lora snickered and nodded. "Oh, yeah. It sounds like some sort of investment: my portfolio includes three CDs, a couple of IRAs, and one STD. Things have gotten awfully complicated, Sue. Marriage was never like this."

It was several hours before the man with whom she had the date Friday called back.

"Do you know, I forgot to get your name?" she said to him.

He laughed briefly over that and then told her he was Thad Morrow.

She liked that, thought it had a nice solid sound to it. They would meet at the front desk in the Hyatt Regency, where he had his reservation, at nine o'clock on Friday evening.

"Should I wear a . . . red flower in my lapel?" he asked. She could hear the smile in his voice.

"Or I could wear a hat with a red flower," she suggested.

"Well, uh, I guess we'll be the ones who are standing around looking for someone. I have dark hair," he said. "Medium build, not fat, not skinny."

"Oh, that helps a lot."

"How about you?" he asked.

"Brown hair, brown eyes, medium build. We certainly sound distinguished. Just your average folks."

He laughed and said, "What will you be wearing?"

"I'll wear a—a—oh, I can't decide on such short notice."

"Hmmm. Just like a woman. Indecisive." His tone was light and inoffensive.

After they hung up, she lost no time in pulling up his records. Or trying to pull them up. There were none. She tried some variant spellings, but she didn't have any luck.

She sighed. Oh, well, he probably let his policy lapse. It often happened, though, that people had old policy information sitting around in a drawer and had long since changed companies. At least she knew his name now.

She smiled to herself, thinking about meeting Thad Morrow. Nice name. It was good to have something to look forward to on Friday night because, while T.G.I.F. and all that, there was something about the prospect of a Friday evening alone that almost put her in a panic. She might have been desperate enough to go to the Neighborhood Watch meeting, and then she would have had to contend with Jack.

30

"I haven't done any canning since Joe died," said Tony's mother, Anna, sitting at her friend Rose's breakfast table. They were having a cup of coffee, heated up from Rose's breakfast. It seemed as if Rose would make a fresh pot now and then, but in all these years, no matter what time of day Anna came over, Rose always just heated up the leftover breakfast coffee. When most people would have left the pot on, Rose turned it off after breakfast, then later heated it up again in a little chipped yellow and black enamel pan dedicated to that purpose. There was a permanent discoloration staining the inside. But far be it from Anna to make any suggestions. It was the company she sought, not the coffee.

"I haven't done any in ages myself," Rose replied, "but I just decided this year I was going to put up some things. But, you know, it's expensive, having to buy the jars and lids and all. I used to have all that stuff, but I guess over the years I just got rid of it." Rose looked vaguely over Anna's shoulder while she searched her memory. "Maybe I gave it away. Seems like maybe Janice took some of my jars to make jelly," she said, referring to her daughter.

"Say," Anna said, "I think I have some jars in the garage. I'm almost sure of it. Joe used to complain about me saving so many. Let's go over and get them for you."

"Well, thanks," Rose replied, getting up to follow Anna, who was already heading toward the front door. "That'd save me a lot of money, if you're sure you're not going to use them."

"I'm sure," Anna answered over her shoulder. "Who would I put anything up for?"

Rose shook her head in sympathy.

"I'll have to find that garage key," Anna mumbled, more to herself than to her friend. "I think it's in the kitchen drawer." The tiny garage could only be entered from the street, even though it looked as if it were attached to the house. The two of them climbed the stoop and Anna fumbled to get the key to the house, which she wore on a chain she dropped down into her cleavage. She tried not to mess up her hair as she pulled the chain from around her neck and over her head.

"Tony here?" Rose asked when they went inside the house.

"No. He must be at his girlfriend's house. I haven't seen him in a couple of days." Her voice took on a whine.

"Anna, you're going to have to encourage him to get out and leave for good. It's not right he should live here forever."

"Well, what's the matter if he wants to live here and take care of his mother? I like to have him here, and it serves his purpose." She sounded cranky with her old friend. She had gotten the door open, and Rose trailed along to the kitchen behind her, where Anna fumbled through a catchall drawer, searching for the key. "When he finds the right girl, he'll move out, I'm sure, but I don't think this one is the right one." She sighed. "He hasn't even brought her over to meet me."

Rose shook her head.

"Here it is," Anna said, producing the key. The two of them went back outside and to the garage. Anna turned the key in the lock and pulled the door open.

"Did Tony trade in his car?" Rose asked.

"I don't think so," Anna said, looking over the gold-colored car in the garage which had prompted her friend's question. "He'd have told me." A frown darkened her face.

"Maybe, maybe not," Rose said. "It seemes to me he just tells you what's convenient for him. It's high time you started treating him like an adult and see that he treats you that way, too."

Anna flushed as she reached for the pull chain for the light. She knew that Rose was alluding to Tony beating her. It hadn't happened often, but Rose had seen the bruises and confronted her. "Don't tell me you bumped into something again," she'd said. "I know exactly where you get all banged up. First you let Joe get away with that, and now Tony. It's sick, Anna."

Anna had responded that it was just his temper and that she had failed as a mother somewhere along the way, which had made Rose snort and put the blame on Joe. Anna had defended him, "Oh, no, Rose, Joe was a good father and a good provider."

They squeezed past the car and to some shelves at the front, where Anna found the boxed-up jars she remembered having and the two of them took them down and carried them back to the driveway, setting them down there so Anna could lock the garage door.

They carried them to Rose's, where they unpacked the boxes and checked the rims of the jars for chips. "I really appreciate this, Anna. It makes me wish I could get started right away."

Anna was feeling a little agitated. "Listen, I better be going."

"What's the rush? He's not there," Rose said, meaning Tony. "You may as well stay and have some lunch with me. I got some salami in the fridge."

"Not today, dear."

Anna went back home and sat down, staring at the wall. It exasperated her when her friend thought she knew what was best. Why didn't she just keep out of it? She didn't know what it was like, being alone. She still had Walter.

What would I do if Tony moved out permanently? she wondered. I would just die of loneliness, that's what. Something is better than nothing. Tears began to glisten in her eyes. Where was Tony? He hadn't come home that morning and he had borrowed all that money. Something was going on. And what was that strange car doing in the garage?

She went to the telephone alcove in the hall and pulled out the directory. Shera's phone number was penciled inside the cover. In case of an emergency, Tony had said. Well, he had taken her emergency money, so maybe this was an emergency. She thought about dialing, then changed her mind, deciding her life had no emergencies anymore. She started back to the living room, then heard a noise. Her heart started pounding as she retraced her steps to the phone. It was probably just the cat, she was sure, but the sound solidified her uneasiness. She picked up the receiver and dialed. It rang several times, then a male voice answered. "I'm trying to reach Tony Longoria," she said. "Is he there?"

31

What could he say about this Tony Longoria's mother? She wasn't really a surprise to Bill because she seemed very much like the young Johnson woman who had been ushered to his desk earlier in the week by Sergeant Maddox. He could have predicted the resemblance. Men picked girlfriends who were replicas of their mothers. Or their opposites. In this case Mrs. Longoria sat fidgeting, her hands in constant motion, just as Shera's had been.

"Can you tell me what has happened to my boy?" she asked after she invited them in.

"You called Shera Johnson's apartment, looking for your son."

He said it as a statement, but she nodded.

"He was her boyfriend?"

"Was?"

"Yes, ma'am, was. Her body was found Tuesday."

Mrs. Longoria drew her breath in sharply.

"When did you last see your son?"

She thought a moment, wondering if there were something she could say to help Tony, but she couldn't think what it would be. "Tuesday, at lunchtime. I fixed him a sandwich."

"Do you know where he is now?"

She shook her head. "I was looking for him at that

girl's place; that's why I called. You don't think . . . he did it?"

"The landlady saw him there that day."

"But why? She was his girlfriend. He wouldn't have done that." Her eyes were brimming with tears.

"Well, we don't know he did it, Mrs. Longoria, but we need to find him. Can you help us?"

"I don't know where he is," she said brokenly. "There's a car in my garage, though. A strange one. Not his. Maybe whoever it belongs to had something to do with it. Maybe they have Tony and his car."

"May we see it?"

She took them to the garage. After a cursory examination of the car, they all went back to the living room and Bill called the lab to send someone over. For evidence, yes, but not for his own satisfaction, because he was already sure. It was Shera's car, and they would find evidence that it had hit the child, a more or less random event that had now escalated.

Shera's visit to the precinct had been late in the afternoon. She must have gone home, slept on what little Bill had told her, then called the insurance woman the following morning. This Tony must have overheard her and started beating her up. Probably not premeditated. But two murders in as many days. What was it doing to him?

Dellasega had gotten information about Tony's car by the time Bill finished his phone call. Maybe they could trace it, figure out where he was.

"Graduation?" asked Dellasega pointing to a framed picture of a boy on top of the television.

Mrs. Longoria nodded.

"How old is he now?" Bill asked.

"Twenty-nine."

Mrs. Longoria pulled a photograph album out from under a lamp table and sat down on the couch with it. "Let me show you what a fine boy he is," she said.

Bill sat down on the edge of the couch beside her. What he saw in the album was an extremely good-looking, dark-haired boy. In one studio shot Tony wore a smile that bordered on detachment; the eyes looked cold. Some people you wouldn't remember, but Bill knew from experience that this one you would. Bill had a picture in his memory of a kid with startling good looks who had confronted him in an alley one day. The kid had the same cold, detached eyes; you looked in them and felt you were looking into an abyss. That one had laid him out with a bullet wound in the chest. He had known that look ever since, and would be more wary. That time, a second too late for his own good, he'd dropped the kid. He hoped never to confront those kind of eyes in a showdown again. But next time he sure as hell would shoot first.

"Handsome boy, Mrs. Longoria," Dellasega said.

"Yes, and he's a good boy. He takes care of me. I mean, a lot of young people would have left home, but Tony has taken care of me since Joe died."

"Joe was your husband?" Bill asked.

Mrs. Longoria nodded.

"Did you know this Shera Johnson?"

"It was just a passing thing," she said, fingering the chain around her neck. "You know. I don't think it would have ever gotten serious. She was probably a sweet girl, but he never brought her home to meet me, so I can't think it was serious."

"Unfortunately, things have gotten serious," Bill said.

"Tony didn't have anything to do with it, I just know," she said, with the blind loyalty of a mother, wringing her hands together in her lap. "We just need to find him and set it all straight. You will be able to find him for me, won't you? I'm just sure someone must have kidnapped him."

Bill hated to think he would have to shatter her illusions. But that would come later. "Do you have a recent picture of him that we could borrow?" he asked.

She raised one hand to her cheek. "I'm afraid not. He hasn't had any made, and I don't have a camera. There might be something in his room," she said vaguely.

"May we look?"

Her concentration seemed to be slipping away. "Oh, certainly. His room is down there." She gestured toward it.

Bill swept his hand back across his hair, thinking how quickly one could get mired, by accident, in life-shattering events. A child running in front of a car could happen to anyone, and then how would most people react? He wasn't sure a lot wouldn't make a run for it. So the guy had a hair-trigger temper, maybe, but so did a lot of people. Yet this Longoria was in up to his neck. He wondered idly if the same thing could happen to him. He thought it odd that he was almost rationalizing the guy's behavior. But he was here with the mother, and he hated to think her boy was bad, really bad. The dissonance of it: her feelings about him contrasting with the person he probably really was.

Damn it, Bill, he said to himself. Don't forget the bastard beat his girlfriend up and stuffed her into a refrigerator. Not to mention the hit-and-run. Bill had interviewed that mother, too, whose child had been killed. He shook his head at his own lapse, and came back to the questioning, which Dellasega had taken over.

"He beat on you, didn't he, Mrs. Longoria?" Dellasega said in his soothing voice.

"No," she answered quickly.

Dellasega just looked at her sympathetically, and Bill kept quiet. The woman began to cry again.

"Who can I call to come over here, Mrs. Longoria?" Dellasega asked.

"My neighbor Rose. She's my friend."

"I'll call her while you look for the picture. Okay?" Dellasega said to Bill, who nodded, and walked down the hallway.

Tony's room was on the left. Bill went in and briefly appraised it. He opened the top dresser drawer, thinking that's where he would keep a picture. His logic was sound; it was full of the miscellany that fills the drawers of life. Scrounging through it, he found a picture of Tony in a uniform. Bill held it between his thumb and forefinger and stared, fixing it in his mind. The face had filled out from the high school picture, but the eyes hadn't gained any humanity. They were still stone cold.

He went back to the living room. "Did you call her neighbor?"

Dellasega nodded.

"I'll meet her outside."

Bill went out the front door, leaving his partner with the woman. Rose was just coming across the street.

"What has happened?"

"My name is Graham." He showed her his badge. "We're looking for Tony Longoria. Before you go in, could you answer a few questions?"

She looked apprehensively toward the house.

"Well, I guess."

"How tall is he?"

"About five foot nine or ten."

"Weight?"

"Just average."

He pulled the picture from his pocket. "Is this a good likeness?"

Rose took the picture and stared at it. Her voice turned hard. "Yes, that's a good likeness. That was when he didn't even come home for his father's funeral. Left his mother to handle it all by herself. What do you think he did?"

"His girlfriend has been murdered and we need to find him for questioning." He paused, then quietly asked, "Does he abuse his mother?"

"She won't tell you so, but yes, sir, he does."

"Thanks for answering my questions. We can go on in."

Now that they knew the name, they could check out his office, his haunts, see if anyone had seen him. Dellasega went to work on that, but Bill went off on another angle.

The neighbor woman's entry into Mrs. Longoria's living room had unleashed a torrent of words, among which Bill heard her say that Tony had taken her sugar-bowl money. Bill had asked how much. When Mrs. Longoria told him, he saw it all, what he would do if he were in Tony's shoes. He had a policeman's hunch and he was going to check it out.

He got on the phone and checked out the flights to Dallas. Then he went to LaGuardia. At the ticket counters, no one remembered his face. "Too many people pass through here," one of them told him. "I don't even look at them." It was a long shot; Tony could have left at any time of the day. But Bill kept at his job methodically.

"Have you ever seen this man? A little older, no uniform?" A thirtyish woman at the fourth gate on his list took the picture from him and squinted, peering at it. "How could I forget someone who looks like that, I ask you? God, he was beautiful," she sighed. "Too bad he was going to Dallas."

"Can you remember when?"

"Yesterday—no, I think the day before. I thought he surely must be a TV leading man or something—on the soaps maybe. But the name wasn't familiar. Joe, I remember that, because it's my father's name. Joe something-or-other."

"You think you can remember the rest?"

"No. I only remember that because of my father. Too many people—"

Bill nodded. "I know." The name didn't matter; names were so easy to change.

Too pretty, the landlady had said, and she had equated it with bad. He could fill in the blanks on this guy's personality. Women came to him, but he was working out some power trip on women like his mother and the girlfriend.

When he got back to work he called Lora.

"Lieutenant Graham here again," he said.

"Oh, hi. Something new?"

"Yeah. The guy. We've got his I.D. Name is Tony Longoria and he's flown to Dallas. That can only mean one thing."

"But how did he—"

"The victim must have left some sort of indication—I guess your number."

"Well, sure. Oh, migosh—"

"What?"

"I've made a date, a blind date, with some man from New York. He just confirmed the time—Friday night—a few minutes ago."

"What'd he say his name was?"

"Thad Morrow."

"How'd he contact you?"

"He called and said he had had a tape deck stolen and wanted to report it."

"It must not be Longoria, then, or you wouldn't have a file."

"I didn't," she said quietly.

"What?"

"When I tried to call it up on the computer, nothing showed up."

"And you still planned to go out with him."

"Well, people forget," she said self-consciously.

"What do you mean?"

"Oh, they change insurers, that sort of thing, and they forget. I thought he had just called the wrong company."

"Do you often go out with strangers?" Immediately he was sorry he asked; it sounded judgmental. He detected the defensiveness in her voice as she told him no, she didn't.

"But I'm divorced and there aren't that many opportunities. . . ." Her voice trailed off.

"I know. I'm single myself."

"What should I do about Friday?"

"We'll intercept him. Where are you meeting? Just tell me the details and I'll let the Dallas police know."

She told him the time and the hotel where they were going to meet.

"Lora, I mean, Ms. Montgomery—" He had been thinking of her as Lora ever since that first call.

"That's okay. Lora."

"Lora, I think I'm going to come down there to handle this."

He found he was disappointed at the completely neutral acceptance of his plan to go to Dallas. Well, what did he expect? He had been fantasizing, but she didn't know anything about it. He remembered one time when Marianne had dreamed that he was making moves on her best friend. When she woke up, she was huffy with him, and it had been several hours before he had coerced her verbally into telling him why. "It was a dream," he had told her. "I'm not responsible for what you dream about me." She agreed, of course, but she still carried herself around with an air of martyrdom for the rest of the day. Dreams, fantasies, he thought—they shouldn't have these qualities of transference.

"Go to Dallas? Not likely, Preacher." The captain was the only one who called him Preacher. Graham hated the nickname, but someone was always coming up with it, ever since the fifties, when he was a kid and was called Billy. Being called a nickname he didn't like still rankled, but now he just acknowledged it with a terse smile, and the name soon died because it didn't fit him. But Captain Frost was one of those kind of people who had to have a nickname for everyone, and he hadn't come up with anything better for Bill. So Preacher it remained, even though he was no preacher and tried to keep his judgments to himself. That was why his remark to Lora had startled him. It had not just sounded judgmental—it had been.

"I'd feel a lot more comfortable about this case if I could handle it personally." He and Dellasega had already briefed the captain.

"I've got a budget to watch over and I don't have any travel money for a junket to Dallas. Not when the Dallas police can handle it." The captain began to shuffle papers around on his desk impatiently.

Bill already had an alternate plan. "Then I'd like to put in for a little of my furlough."

The captain looked at him with his head cocked to one side. He squinted his eyes and said, "What's really going down in Dallas?"

Bill felt the color begin to rise in his face. "Nothing. I just feel like I'm trying to operate one of those damn bucket loaders in a glass case at the carnival, and I don't like it. I don't want to come up with an empty bucket. I want to go after this guy."

The captain studied him for a moment with a frown, then nodded. "You can have a furlough. Turn in the paperwork."

32

Serena pulled out of the driveway, waving her fingertips briefly at Martin, who stood in the doorway to Lora's house. They had interrupted their tryst so she could get back to work on time—well, almost on time. She glanced at her watch. She was already late. Martin had stayed behind to make sure there were no traces of their rendezvous.

Serena felt a smile play at her lips. That Martin. He had called her at work and insisted she meet him for lunch at his ex-wife's. Ha! she thought, what a lunch. She hoped he knew what he was doing, having them meet there. He assured her it was okay, that he wanted to see her and

Lora's was . . . was convenient, what else? They didn't have time to go to their own places during the lunch hour.

She put the car in gear and eased down the street. She felt mellow; she and Martin had a few hits on a joint he'd bought off a guy at work, then had made love. Much better than last night. She was glad she had agreed to meet him. She ran her hand under her hair and lifted it off her neck, letting the spring breeze tickle it.

She loved Martin. She didn't tell him that, though, because she figured it might scare him. He was still in the post-divorce trauma stage.

She was beyond that now, and picking another possible mate was a deliberate process. There weren't many acceptable men around. When she was eighteen, she had married Leon based on physical attraction, feeling certain that not only would it last, but that everything else would fall into place. Their love could surmount the fact that he was from a different kind of background. Their love could surmount the fact that neither of them could stand the other's families. Their love could surmount anything, even Leon's lack of ambition. Well, three kids later, the debits had added up and put their relationship in the red. Now she was much more critical. She didn't know if she could chalk her disillusionment up to experience, growing wisdom, or just plain cynicism. Perhaps wisdom was tempered with cynicism.

She had lots of male friends, and they were just that, friends. The guys at work, that sort of thing. But she wouldn't give two hoots to marry most of them, even if they were available. Men got sloppy, not just around the house, but their habits—farting, burping without any "excuse me," picking their noses, and scratching their asses. Self-absorbed. They all seemed to be self-absorbed.

Then she had met Martin, and he seemed, well, presentable at least. And even tempered. He had a certain amount of common sense and seemed to be able to look at things reasonably. He was a big help around the house, too. Just little things, like helping her clear the table after dinner. She wondered if he had always been like that or whether being single had helped. This would be the first time he had ever lived on his own, without a woman to take care of him. That helped a man, it seemed to her.

He was acceptable. It wasn't a great love, but then maybe that only happens the first time, when all the illusions of youth are in place. Fifteen years of marriage, three kids, and Leon had pretty much milked her of her illusions.

She didn't know why she hinted to Martin that she might remarry Leon. She wouldn't even consider it. Not that it wasn't true that she was tired of going it alone. But Leon wasn't a possibility. She had only said it out of some little bit of perversity in her personality, maybe to bring Martin to attention.

She pulled up at a stop sign and glanced in the rearview mirror. Adrenaline shot through her at the sight of a man's face staring back at her.

"I have a knife, so don't scream," he said softly, right into her ear.

She shook her head, indicating she wouldn't.

The soft voice continued: "Turn right here and just drive till I tell you where to turn."

The knife was at her throat now; she could feel the thin blade, his proof that he wasn't bluffing. It was a woman's worst nightmare coming true, but it was broad daylight. It wasn't happening in the dead of night; there were people all around, people watering their yards. There was a woman getting her mail out of the mailbox. She had read about things like this, but they had seemed such remote possibilities. The only time she was ever scared was when she awoke to a strange sound in the night, one that preceded consciousness. But here was horror abroad in the daytime. And she, Serena Wilks, who tried to be a good person, was going to be its victim.

She found herself thinking that she shouldn't have violated Lora's house, that she was being punished.

She drove into the country, just as he ordered, until he told her to turn down a lane that didn't appear to go anywhere. They were at the midline of two fields.

He'll rape me, but I can live through that, she thought. Please, dear God, just don't let him kill me. She remembered reading somewhere that you shouldn't fight a rapist, just be passive. It was a power thing. Just let him have his way. Well, she would do that. Whatever was necessary to survive. But what, dear God, *was* that?

He ordered her to stop and get out of the car, which she did. He got out, too, then grabbed her by the wrist. She looked at the knife, which he had in one hand. Shit, she thought, it was just a dinky little pocket knife. I should have made a break for it.

He shoved her into the backseat, but he didn't rape her. Instead, his hands closed around her neck and pressed harder and harder. She was gasping for air, then the air inside her couldn't get out. She was going to explode.

Just as blackness began to come, she heard a faraway voice say: "You can't tell on me now, Lora."

33

Bart and Lonnie weren't there when he got back, so Tony got himself a wine cooler out of the refrigerator, took it into the living room and turned on the radio. He walked around the room, looking in the bookshelves, getting a bead on what kind of guy Bart was. It was hard, though; he had a little of everything. The hourly news came on, but Tony wasn't paying much attention till he heard them say something about a woman being assaulted northwest of Dallas. It was the "left for dead" that shocked him. But the shock continued. The victim had been identified as Serena Wilks.

"Goddamn, fuckin' slitch. The goddamn rotten whore." Invectives were rolling off his tongue, expressing his dismay that he could have gotten the wrong person again. "Why can't they goddamn be who they're supposed to be, be where they're supposed to be." He was throwing things now. First the pillows, then his bottle slammed into the wall, spewing its contents. An ashtray full of cigarette butts. He hurled all the magazines off the coffee table, then kicked the table over.

The tirade lasted only a brief time. Then he got a glazed look on his face and sat down on the couch to think. There couldn't be any more screw-ups. He sat there a moment, a grimace contorting his features, as the memory of his father came to him.

"You are a screw-up, boy. Everything you do, you screw it up." He was holding him by the collar, the side of it cutting into his neck. He was fourteen and had been suspended from school for fighting, and his mother had informed dad as soon as the old man came in the door. She always sided with him, even though he beat the crap out of her weekly.

He was sitting on the bed when his father came into his room. "Your mama tells me you been fighting."

He just stared at his father, injudiciously, like a typical adolescent, and didn't say anything.

"What was it about?"

Reluctantly Tony said that a kid had called him a queer.

"Did you tear his balls off?"

Tony looked down nervously.

"You let him win, didn't you? Because you are a queer, just like he said. You pretty boy," he said in a contemptuous tone, "you aren't tough enough." His father grabbed him up and threw him against the wall. "You're a screw-up, boy. You'll never be a man unless them punk kids beat it into you. How in hell did I get such a pussy for a son? I think your mama must have been ballin' the goddamn milkman."

Tony's face twisted with the memory, then he let loose another tirade, this one with the sound of anguish in his voice.

"What in the hell was she doing at Lora's house?"

He had been casing the neighborhood, had just spotted Lora's house number when he saw a man drive up, unlock the door and go in. Then, as he pulled through the cul-de-sac, a woman came along, parked next to the man's car and went inside, too. Home for lunch, he guessed.

He had assumed it was Lora. A screw-up, boy. Well, who the hell were those people in her house? Must have been Lora's old man, and he had a little something going on the side.

Christ, he had tried to be careful. He had made sure all the blinds were closed in the house before he got out of the car. He had been careful about that. He had watched the neighbors' places to make sure no one was watching. But their blinds were all closed. He'd been careful about that. It was lonely out there, as if he were the only living soul in the world, but he knew there were two people in that house on the cul-de-sac. He'd parked down the way a little, so he went back and climbed into *her* car, an older-model station wagon, and pulled the door closed almost silently. It was a good place to hide because the backseat was full of all kinds of family crap—a baby car seat, towels, several pair of sneakers, and Cheerios, strewn all over the floor. Then he just got down and waited. After a while he heard another car. The door slammed on it, maybe across the street. He thought he was going to have to wait forever, hunkered down, his legs cramped, but finally she came out and he heard her say good-bye to the man and "See you, tonight." With any luck, no, Tony thought.

But, goddamn, it wasn't Lora.

Well, they both deserved it, she and the other one; they were both whores. Sleeping with anyone. The last one, she hadn't even put up a fight. She hadn't even tried to fight him off or plead with him. And the other one, she was asking for whatever she got, willing to do anything he wanted. The world was better off without them.

He began to pick up the mess he had made, hoping the table wasn't damaged. He went to the kitchen and got a wet rag to clean up the rug. It was going to be hard to explain why he had thrown his drink. He'd think of something or, fuck, he'd kill the damn fags. What did it matter now?

34

They were all in a state of shock.

The supervisor had called an unscheduled staff meeting thirty minutes earlier and had told them that L.J. Andrews had been murdered. Her sister had found her after not being able to reach her since Tuesday. The news was met with a few exclamations and then silence, as they all tried to take it in. Now they were going through their routines perfunctorily, but murder doesn't happen so close without a stunning effect.

"I feel like an ogre for not being nicer to her," Sue said to Lora when they went on break.

"I know what you mean."

"There was no convincing her that picking up guys in bars was dangerous. She thought she could tell the good guys from the bad."

"You think it was someone she picked up?"

"Well, what do you think?" Sue answered.

"I guess that will be the general assumption of everyone

here, but maybe she surprised a burglar or something like that."

"Maybe," Sue said, but she didn't sound convinced.

Lora had no sooner gotten her head set back on than her extension rang. "Lora," Martin said, "I need help." He sounded distraught.

"What is it?"

"Someone tried to kill Serena. She's in intensive care, and I've got to get over there and see how she is."

"Where are you?"

"At the police station for questioning." His voice broke as he said, "They think I did it. Why would I do it? I love her. How can they think that?"

"Oh, Martin, I'm so sorry. What can I do?"

"Get hold of a lawyer; I think I'm gonna need one. I've got to get out of here and go to the hospital. I don't want her to wake up alone there."

"How about her relatives? Does she have any?"

"No. Her folks are dead. There's just the kids and Leon." He sounded disgruntled. "They called him when they identified her."

"Where are the kids?" she asked, using practicality to hide her dismay.

"They're all right. They're with Leon now. Isn't that guy across the street from you a lawyer?"

"Yes, but I don't know how good."

"Well, I need to get out of here. He'll know what to do."

"Martin, you've got to tell me more about what happened."

"They found her on a road west of here just after one today. Someone had strangled her, but she wasn't dead. Thank God." Again he choked up. When he recovered, he said, "Listen, I gotta go. I'll tell you everything later. Just get me a lawyer."

"Okay." She couldn't believe it. Was it a practical joke? But he wouldn't joke about Serena being in the hospital.

Lora went to her supervisor and explained the situation as best she could. The supervisor said she could make up the time.

She grabbed her purse, locked her desk, and stopped by to briefly tell Sue what was going on.

"This is unbelievable; I feel as if I'm in a nightmare," Lora told her. "First L.J., now this." She shook her head in disbelief. "You let me know if I can be of any help."

"Thanks."

35

Sue frowned as her friend walked out of the office. Lora had told her earlier about how the police thought the blind date she had was with—what did they call it?—the perpetrator. It was like a soap opera. No sooner had Lora disappeared down the hall than her extension buzzed. Sue answered it.

"I was trying to reach Lora Montgomery. Is she there?"

"I'm sorry, she's gone for the afternoon," Sue said, thinking the voice sounded familiar. "May I help you?"

The caller hesitated, then said, "It's urgent that I reach

her. I'm calling from the police about a call she received earlier in the week.''

''Is this Lieutenant Graham? I thought I recognized your accent. This is Sue Evans. I talked to you the other day.''

''Oh, yes. How are you?''

''Just fine, thanks.''

''Do you think I could reach Lora at home?''

''I doubt it. You see, this dreadful thing has happened. Her ex-husband has been arrested for attempted murder. They think he tried to strangle his girlfriend. There's no way that's true—I've only met him once, but he's no murderer. If you pull any weight with the police down here . . .''

''I'll do my best to help. And meanwhile, would you know when I *could* reach Ms. Montgomery?''

''I guess the best time to get her will be tomorrow here at work.''

He paused, as if deciding how much to say to Sue, then: ''Has she told you about the call she received earlier in the week?''

''Yes. She told me all about your phone call to her—how you all think this blind date she has tomorrow night is with the murderer. I was suspicious of that from the very minute I heard about it.''

''You sound very astute.''

Sue chuckled. ''I'm afraid my old man calls it being a busybody.''

''Listen, I appreciate your help.''

''Thanks,'' Sue said.

''I guess I'm out of luck today, so I'll just try tomorrow.''

''Sure. Well, she'll be here. Life may be falling apart around her, but Lora still gets to work. She's what you'd call reliable.''

36

Lora knew where Jack's office was, so she drove by.

Jack's secretary was attractive in a cheap sort of way. A little too much makeup—the eyes overdrawn—the hair a little too unkempt for a professional office. Lora imagined, though, that Jack liked to look at her because she exuded youth and sexuality.

"He's not in just now," the secretary purred in an undiscriminatingly seductive voice as she quickly shut her drawer on whatever she'd been doing when Lora came in. Probably reading a book.

"I'm his neighbor; I live right across the street, and I need to reach him as soon as possible."

"Well, I normally don't tell people that he's at the golf course, but that's where he is. He left here about noon. He should probably be getting through pretty soon." She glanced at her watch.

"Will he come back here?"

"No, he'll just go home or wherever."

"Okay. Thanks."

Poor Martin. I'm not getting him out of there very quickly, she thought as she waited impatiently at her house for Jack to return home. She realized that she was reacting as though Martin was part of her family. Well, wasn't he? How long would it be before she stopped seeing him in the blacks and whites of love? After all, she had spent seventeen years of her life caring about him, and one couldn't just turn that off overnight.

They had met at Oklahoma State University, where she was majoring in business and he in engineering. When he graduated, she had quit school to marry him and they moved to Oklahoma City. She had always imagined she would work a year or so, get pregnant and have a family. But it hadn't worked out that way, and she had spent seven years as a secretary for a CPA. She was ready when, ten years ago, Martin had suggested they migrate to Texas, to the Dallas-Fort Worth area, where the economy was booming. Eighteen months ago Martin had decided to change jobs again—a fateful move, she thought, looking back on it, because it was this last job where he had met the other woman.

Eager to change everything associated with her marriage, Lora had moved from a bedroom community between Dallas and Fort Worth to an apartment at the edge of Dallas, and then to her house. Finally, she had quit her job. With a set of good recommendations, it hadn't taken her long to find another, the one at UACA. The job change, which was motivated by the divorce, had been a good one. In addition to a better salary, UACA had a good benefits package including a profit-sharing plan, which seemed vitally more important to her now, as a single woman. The future had a different cast to her without Martin.

Lora was sitting on a bar stool, gazing toward the front of the house in a reverie, when she saw Jack's car drive in. She jumped down and hurried out and across the street.

"Well, hon, that's the best reception I've ever had from you. That'll make up for my poor game today."

"My ex-husband is in jail and he doesn't think it looks good. Can you help?" At Jack's frown, she continued, "He's been arrested. His girlfriend was assaulted and they think he did it."

"Has he actually been arrested or are they just questioning him?"

"I'm not sure. He just said to get him a lawyer and come down to police headquarters."

"What about the girlfriend?" Jack asked.

"She's unconscious. God, I hope she's going to be okay." Lora paused. "She could clear him. But if she doesn't regain consciousness . . ."

"Hmmm. What time did this assault happen?" Jack asked.

"Around noon or one, maybe."

"Well, I may have something that will help. I saw him leave your place after one. I was just getting ready to leave for my golf game."

"My place?" She looked perplexed. "What was he doing there?"

"Hon, I hate to tell you, but he met a woman over there. I saw her leave, too, but a few minutes before him. One thing's for sure, they didn't leave together."

Any other time, Lora might have been angry with Martin for using her house for an assignation, but the gravity of the present situation eclipsed ordinary feelings, putting things in a different perspective. She only felt astonished at his lack of sensitivity.

"Will you go down there with me?"

"You bet. I'll drive; you go around and climb in."

"I just can't believe he met her at my house."

"If they were screwing around, then there's evidence that he was with her, so I can see why they picked him up. Lucky thing I saw them. That'll at least confirm his story."

Lora nodded.

Jack's story did help, and the timing was corroborated by one of Martin's co-workers. The time it had taken Martin to drive from Lora's house to his office didn't allow for anything but a direct trip.

The police released Martin and the three of them walked to Jack's car. "I need to get to the hospital. Will you take me by there?" he asked Jack.

"They're not going to let you in to see her."

"I know, but I'd like to be there, nearby, when she comes to."

It must be love, Lora thought, since Martin hated hospitals yet wanted to wait in one. "Why don't you come by my place, Martin, and I'll give you something to eat, then I'll take you to get your car? What did they do, pick you up at work?"

"Yeah. I couldn't eat now, but I guess I should have my car."

When they reached Lora's, Martin thanked Jack, telling him to send him a bill for his time.

"Don't worry about it. I did it to be neighborly. Neighborhood watch, right?" It was not what he said, but how he said it, looking beyond Martin and at her, that bothered Lora. The "neighborly" carried an implication she didn't like. But he had been helpful, there was no doubt, and he'd never really done anything except make innuendos. She was glad, at least, of that.

She and Martin went into her house and she convinced him that he needed to eat something, so he sat down at the bar while she opened canned vegetable soup, poured it in a pan to heat, then began to make bologna sandwiches.

"This has really brought me around," he said as she prepared the lunch.

"I guess so."

"You know, Lora, I really appreciate your helping me out. I mean, I know you don't owe me any favors."

She shrugged. "You know I care what happens to you."

After a while he said, "Our marriage wasn't bad, was it?"

"You know I didn't think so, Martin."

"I didn't either, till one day I began to get this feeling that I might die and never have lived—you know, *really* lived. I had this incredible feeling of impending doom."

Lora handed their full soup bowls and sandwiches across the bar to Martin, who automatically took them to the table. Then, carrying drinks and spoons, she came into the dining area.

"The fallacy is," he continued, "that I didn't die. I made a life decision based on the feeling, and then I had to live with it."

"It's funny, too," she added, "how we can't learn by anyone else's experience. I've run into so many people who've had almost identical experiences to ours. I've even read about them. But people keep on making the same mistakes."

"Yeah," he agreed, but went on quickly, as if he weren't really listening to her. "I just felt hopelessly compelled to get a divorce because I was in love and I might miss out on something."

"Not everything about our relationship was healthy, though," she said, thinking about how he often had failed to listen to her.

"No, I know that. But it was better than a lot."

She nodded. "How about you and Serena?"

"That's a funny thing. I had just about decided to ask her to marry me, then this happened. And I regret not getting around to it. What if something happens to her?" His voice broke.

"You're sure it's not just the crisis, the impending feeling of doom you were talking about?"

"No, I realized last night just how much she's come to mean to me. This has just emphasized it."

Lora felt a funny little constriction in her chest. This was Martin speaking, the man she had loved, with whom she had lived for years and had expected to spend the rest of her life. She didn't want to remarry him, and yet . . . She stood up and excused herself to refill their glasses, so he wouldn't see the tears beginning to form.

Later, after she had taken him to his car and she was alone, she had a good cry. A bit of mourning for something passing permanently, a bit of grief for something gone.

37

Bart and Lonnie found Tony sitting in the darkened living room when they came in from dinner. They had asked him to go out to dinner with them earlier, but he'd refused.

"You look like you lost your best friend," Bart said to

him, snapping on a small lamp. "I've got the cure for that." He disappeared for a moment and came back with a small plastic bag of marijuana and a package of cigarette papers. He kicked his shoes off, then flopped down on the floor. Lonnie sat down beside him, pulling a pillow off the couch to lean on.

"Join us, Joe," he told Tony.

That's what I need, Tony thought.

Bart and Lonnie shared a joint, while Tony rolled his own. Bart got up and put some music on, then came and sat beside Tony, who was leaning against the couch. None of them said much; they just smoked, waiting for the placid feeling of well-being to steal over them. Lonnie didn't smoke much because he had an appointment, and he soon excused himself and left.

Tony hardly noticed; he was in another world, where he felt warm, loved, and loving. Life had no imperatives. Time had ceased to be of any importance, and he was enjoying the languid feeling the drug was producing. The heady smell of the smoke permeated the air around him.

Bart was sitting with his eyes shut, appearing to savor each drag on the joint. He lazily moved his leg over against Tony's, then began to move it slightly.

Tony noticed a stirring in him, a prelude to arousal. He enjoyed the feeling for a moment, letting it wash over him and grow, until some inner voice asserted itself. Then he moved his leg away and murmured, "You gay son of a bitch. Leave me alone."

Bart smiled lazily. "Relax, man."

"Shit," Tony said, pulling himself up. He started to drop the joint in an ashtray, then decided to keep it for later, when he was alone.

"Hey, nothing happened. You don't have to leave," Bart said with a crooked grin on his face.

Tony was already on his way up to his room. To him something had happened: he was aroused. It scared the hell out of him, even high.

38

"So, I guess it's over for sure with Martin and me now." Lora was bringing Sue up to date over morning coffee in the lounge.

"You've felt that anyway, haven't you?"

"Yes, but now it seems more final."

"Not if Serena doesn't recover."

"Don't even say that, Sue."

Sue shrugged. "Sorry. The cops called here yesterday, looking for you."

"Oh, really? They didn't ever get me. I wonder what they wanted."

"It was that New York one, Lieutenant Graham."

"Oh. I thought you meant the Dallas police. That other thing has just about been pushed out of my head by Martin's problems."

"Not for long. That blind date is tonight."

"Yes, but I don't have to go."

"Don't you kind of want to? To be in on the action? You said your life was blah—well, here's your big chance."

"This wasn't exactly what I had in mind."

They talked about both incidents some more, then returned to their desks. A local call came through for Lora just as she got her headset on. It was Lieutenant Graham.

"I'm in Dallas now, at police headquarters. They checked out this guy you have the date with. This, uh . . ." He paused as if consulting something, then continued, "Thad Morrow. He isn't registered at the Hyatt."

"I can't believe it," she said. "He sounded so nice."

"You can't trust how someone sounds, you should know that."

She bristled slightly. "How should I know that? I've always been a very good judge of people's characters."

He laughed. "I'm sorry. I didn't mean to impugn your judgment. I seem to keep putting my foot in my mouth with you."

"What do you mean?" she asked, not remembering another time.

"The other day. I sounded critical when I asked if you often went out with strangers."

"Oh, that." She remembered. "Well, I really know it isn't a good practice. I think I've just been grasping at straws lately."

"What do you mean?"

"Oh, forget it. It's just my personal life. In a shambles."

"In what way?"

"Lieutenant Graham, is this a business call or what?"

"Oh, yeah, sorry. I need to get a picture of this Longoria back from the local police to bring to show you."

"That's okay. I won't need to know what he looks like." A frown formed on her forehead. "Will I?"

"The local police think you need to be at the Hyatt tonight just like you said you'd be. So nothing goes wrong."

"I was afraid that was what you were going to say. Is it really necessary?"

"Don't worry. We'll be there. We just don't want to foul this up."

"Well, all right. If you really think I need to. My friend here at work was saying I ought to get in on the action, so I guess I am, huh?" They arranged for him to pick her up that evening, and she described how to get to her house. "Isn't it kind of unusual for a policeman to come across the country on a case? Or is it just a myth—this tight budget stuff we hear?"

"No, it's no myth. I—I—just like to finish what I start. Closure, I think they call it. However, this is technically my vacation."

"You are dedicated."

"Crazy, maybe."

"No, not crazy, I'm sure," she said thoughtfully. She had an inordinate desire to keep talking to this man.

"I have a brother in Waxahachie."

"So you came to visit; that explains it." She could have stopped there, but didn't want to end the conversation, so she went on quickly: "I've been down there. Went down when they were filming that movie, *Places in the Heart*."

"A groupie, Lord help me."

She smiled. "I think I could be if it weren't so—so—"

"Unsophisticated."

"For want of a better word. Listen, I grew up on *Photoplay* and *Modern Screen*."

"I went in more for *Plastic Man* and *Captain Marvel* myself."

"My brother liked those."

"Where did you grow up?" he asked.

"Oklahoma." She leaned on her elbow and began to fiddle with a strand of hair behind her ear.

"An Okie."

How curious, she thought. This man was interested in her, she could feel it. Not just in the case, but in her personally. Her female sensors for that sort of thing were up and working, signaling something between them. And there was no question about it. The feeling was there, very present, even over the phone.

"Yes. And you're a New Yorker."

"Except for, like I told you, when I was in the Army in El Paso for a while." Oh, yes, she remembered. And he also had told her he was single. "You know, it was embarrassing having to confess that I had made that date with a complete stranger."

"Do you date a lot?"

She laughed. "One real date in a year. A lot."

"What constitutes a real date?"

"You get invited to go somewhere. He pays. Like the old days."

"Oh, I see."

She could hear the smile in his voice.

"Are you divorced?" he asked.

"Yes."

"I haven't dated much either. It seems too fraught with danger."

She laughed. "Danger?"

"Might fall in love."

"Would that be bad?"

"You can get hurt," he said.

"True, but it does get lonely."

"Oh, yes, it does," he agreed. "Any children?"

"No," she said, almost apologetically. "You?"

"I have a boy, Patrick."

"I bet that made the divorce especially hard."

"Divorce is hard no matter what."

There was a pause while she wondered where to turn the conversation. They both started to say something at the same time, then stopped, tried again.

"You first," he said.

"No, you," she answered, laughing.

"When this is over . . . well, I'm going to be around for a few days at least. Maybe I could take you on a real date. Maybe this weekend. This is your city; maybe you could show me some of the sights."

"Do I know you well enough?" she said with mock concern.

"I could give you references."

She smiled and said, "It's a date. After tonight."

Later, at her desk, Sue passed by and asked, "Well, how'd it go?"

"I've got to go to the Hyatt tonight and meet that guy."

"No kidding." Sue frowned. "You be careful."

"This is what you wanted me to do, isn't it? Get into the excitement?"

"Well, I still want you to be careful."

"I'm sure there's no danger. I mean, the police will be there." She meant it, but still felt nervous.

39

Sue pushed a lock of hair away from her forehead with the back of her wrist. She was standing at the sink, doing the last of the dinner dishes—it was her turn—and her hands were drippy. She glanced at the kitchen clock: almost eight, reminding her that Lora would be going to the Hyatt soon; she might be on her way now. What a bizarre week it had been.

After she put the last of the dishes in the drainer, she hung the dishcloth on a rack, dried her hands, and went into the living room. Kevin was sitting on the couch, watching TV. "You know, Kevin, I'm kind of worried about Lora."

"How come?" he asked, his eyes remaining riveted to the television screen.

"I don't know, just a gut level feeling." She had already filled Kevin in on Lora's situation.

"Did you see the note I left you?

"What note?"

"To call her. She called while you were at the store."

"Why didn't you tell me?"

"I forgot. That's why I wrote it down. I left it on the note pad by the phone. I thought you'd see it."

She walked over to the telephone. There was Kevin's note. *Call Laura.*

"That's it, Kevin!"

"What's it?" Her exclamation finally got his full attention, and he looked away from the TV.

She had torn the page off the note pad. "Lora, Laura." She was careful to pronounce them as they should be. "Whoever killed L.J. meant to kill Lora."

"Oh, c'mon, Sue. Don't you think your imagination is getting carried away?"

"No, Kevin, you don't understand. You see, L.J. is really Laura Jean. Get it?"

He began to nod with comprehension, and Sue went on: "This many things simply don't happen in one week by coincidence to one person. I'm thinking about Martin's girlfriend, too.''

''You do have a point. It is a bit unlikely. If you take anyone else as a focal point, there is no pattern, is there? None of it fits together in a meaningful way.''

''But if you start with Lora as the focal point,'' Sue said, picking up his line of thought, ''the other seemingly random events fall into kind of an order. I think I'd better call her. I don't know what bearing this has on the guy supposedly waiting for her at the Hyatt, but . . .''

40

A maroon Toronado pulled up in front of Lora's house, and she saw a man get out. She had been wandering nervously through the house, unable to settle down to anything, waiting to go to the Hyatt for the rendezvous.

By the time the man reached the house, she had the door open. She extended her hand. ''Lieutenant Graham?'' He seemed vaguely familiar to her, and she momentarily wondered why.

He took her hand. ''And you're Lora.''

She felt the sexual electricity flow between them at his touch. Suddenly she felt shy and uncertain—but one of the advantages of age, she realized, is that experience has taught you how to press onward anyway. ''After our phone conversation,'' she said, ''I feel like I know you.'' Still they held on to each other. The charge in the air required nothing else, but it didn't hurt that he was also attractive, that there were no visible flaws.

"Shall we go?" she said, glancing at her watch. "I've been ready for quite a while—I'm so nervous. It's not every day you have an appointment with a—a murderer. What if I can't act normal and he suspects something?"

"You'll be fine," he said, his tone caressing her with its concern, "and I'll be there to take care of you."

"Lora." He dropped her hand and stepped back. It was Helen Myers, her next door neighbor. "Sorry to interrupt you, but can I get you to water my plants and pick up the mail this week? We're leaving for my mother's tonight. We're hoping Janet will sleep—that little monster—she's a terrible traveler." She gave a little laugh. "We should be back next Sunday."

"Sure, Helen, I'd be glad to." Lora took the key her neighbor was extending.

"I'm glad I caught you," the neighbor said. "You look like you're on your way out. Say, are you okay? You look a little peaked."

"I'm all right. I've just had a bad week," Lora replied. She didn't know Helen well enough to want to tell her about Serena, nor about her impending date.

"Well, I usually water the plants in the middle of the week. I put them all in the kitchen to make it easier for you. And just stack the mail anywhere."

"I'll take care of it, Helen. Don't worry, just have a good trip," she said, calling after her neighbor, who was already loping toward home. "Just a moment while I put this up," she said, holding up the key. She went inside and put it in an ashtray on the stereo, but before she could return to the porch, the phone rang. "We may never get away," she called outside. "Come on in, if you want to, while I answer that."

She was surprised to hear Sue's voice on the other end of the line.

41

"Mrs. Wilks has regained consciousness," the policeman said to him. "She asked to see you. They said you can go in." Martin felt tears burn his eyes. "Just for a moment, though."

He went to her bedside, where they had tubes and monitors strung to her. "Serena, I'm here."

She opened her eyes and focused on him. "Martin." She lifted her hand weakly and he took it.

"I love you, Serena."

A brief smile flitted across her lips. "Good to hear," she said in a tired whisper.

"Who did this to you, Serena? We've got to get him."

"Don't know. I . . . seem to be . . . jinxed. Coincidence . . . or something." Her talk was labored.

"What do you mean?"

Again the brief smile appeared. Serena's incomparable nature showing itself even now, Martin thought. "He . . ." She paused for a moment. ". . . called me . . . Lora. Can you . . . believe it?" She gave his hand a little good-natured squeeze, but Martin didn't find it at all humorous. The more he pondered it, the less he thought it was coincidence. On the way to get his car the night before, Lora had told him all about the situation she was involved in. This had to be the same guy.

When the nurse made him leave, he found his way to a bay of telephones. He picked up the receiver after checking the directory and started to dial the police, then hung up and rehearsed what he would tell them.

This is Martin Montgomery. You had me down there, questioning me about the assault of my girlfriend, and she's regained consciousness and told me her attacker mistakenly called her Lora. That's my wife's name. And there's this guy from New York who's stalking her, so I think whoever attacked my girlfriend probably meant to attack Lora, because Serena was in Lora's house.

Too preposterous? It meant that the guy had been in town since at least noon of yesterday.

He was holding the receiver again, undecided about what to do, whom to call. He dialed Lora's number, but the line was busy. If he only knew at which hotel she was meeting that guy, he would go over there. But he didn't. He hung up, deciding to go to Lora's house. He'd have just enough time to go to her place, talk to her, then get back to see Serena again in an hour.

42

"Did you know the woman who was killed, Brad?"

"Uh-huh," Brad murmured, running his tongue along Tracy's earlobe, letting it dart into her ear, then back, teasingly.

"Very well?"

"Christ, Tracy, do you have to talk about it now? I mean, talking about a dead person kind of spoils the mood, you know?"

"Well, I just wondered," the woman said, stretching under him. "Did you ever go out with her?"

Brad had been wrapped over her, one leg across her thighs, but now he rolled away and sighed heavily. "Yeah, once or twice a long time ago."

"Was she pretty?"

"Hell, Tracy, you've seen her. She was the one we saw the other night at Angelo's, coming out the door when we went in."

Tracy sat up, her breasts dropping heavily at the sudden motion. "That must have been the very night she was killed. Do you suppose . . ."

Brad sat up, too. "Yes, I do suppose. Shit. What was that guy's name? He'd been in to UACA that day to apply for a job. I've got an application on him.'' His voice had risen in excitement and he bent over and started pulling on his socks. "Come on. Get dressed. I gotta go over there and get the file.''

43

"C'mon, man, I'll pay you back by tomorrow, no shit.''

Jerry Joe Lansing was trying to freeload some cocaine off his friend. He had spotted him sitting in his usual place at a drive-in restaurant and slid into the front seat beside him.

"Fuck off, J.J. You still owe me for last time. If you wasn't my friend, I'd a kicked your ass by now.''

The rejection made Jerry Joe's temper flare. "You goddamn prick,'' he said, slammed the door and went back to his own car—a blue Skylark, patchworked with dabs of primer. He would have like to have roared away, but the car wouldn't start the first time and he had to sit there till it finally turned over.

He'd calmed down by the time he reached his house, but in place of the outburst was a cold determination. He took the stairs to the bedrooms two at a time, and instead of going into his own, went into his brother's room. Flipping on the light, he went over to the chest of drawers. He slid the second drawer open and plunged his hand underneath the rumple of underwear, coming up with what to him was a plum: his brother's Saturday Night Special.

44

"That was my friend Sue on the phone—remember? You talked to her yesterday. She thinks that there's a connection between me and this woman at work who got murdered. Do you know about that? You see, her name was Laura, L-A-U-R-A, and I'm L-O-R-A, so she went by L.J. to keep things from getting confused. Speaking of which—" They were in the car, pulling away from the curb, and Lora realized she was talking a mile a minute, so she abruptly halted her commentary with a deep audible breath. "Lieutenant Graham, you'll have to forgive me. I'm really keyed up."

His smile transcended the waning light as he reached over and gave her shoulder a squeeze. "You don't need to be afraid," he said, and his voice gave her confidence. Besides, was it fear she was feeling, or just excitement? Excitement over what was yet to come, but also by his sheer physical presence. Could he be feeling it, too? she wondered. They were easing toward the corner stop sign. "Listen, you're going to have to give me directions," he said, "I'm a stranger, remember?"

She could feel the warmth of his hand through her blouse. "Two left turns, then a right," she said, recalling the last time she had given those directions—to Brad. Funny how things could change so quickly; to think she had been wishing Brad would ask her out less than a week ago. "You aren't exactly what I expected," she said, returning her attention to the present.

"What did you expect?"

"Oh, maybe a Barney Miller type."

"I'm not that," he said, smiling.

"No, you're not that."

"Disappointed?" he asked.

"Well," she said hesitantly, "it's not my business to be disappointed or not disappointed."

He smiled, and as he made the first turn, she began having an internal argument with herself about whether to be bold—as L.J. would have been—and take control of this situation aggressively, or to be ladylike and demure, leaving everything to chance.

Bold won, and she said, "I wish we didn't have to go to the Hyatt," but her voice didn't reflect what she meant. He turned to look briefly at her and said, "Don't worry. It's just something we've got to do."

"I'm not worried. I meant that instead of the Hyatt we could go somewhere else, like we talked about, on a 'real' date."

He nodded, and she found herself wondering if she had imagined his interest in her. But could this exaggerated physical reaction be one-sided? She took a deep breath and closed her eyes to get control. Come back to earth, Lora, she told herself, you're going to scare him off.

They drove in silence for a few minutes, then he abruptly steered the car onto the shoulder of the road, stopped the engine, and without prelude pulled her over to him and kissed her, long and hard. She was surprised at the taste of blood where her teeth had pressed against the insides of her lips and almost didn't hear his breathless words murmured against her hair— "goddamned sexy slitch." Her heart lurched as she remembered where she had heard that word before—over the phone line as the man beat up on the woman who had called. But surely it was simply a coincidence.

This man's a policeman, for God's sake, here to protect me, she thought. Why would he call her that name? He couldn't be the man; the suspect was at the Hyatt. Wasn't he? With a sudden chill, she realized she hadn't even asked to see this man's identification; she'd been too taken with his looks and his air of legitimacy.

He abruptly pulled away from her and muttered, "Migod." He gripped the steering wheel and she sat back, watching him in the dim light from the dashboard. I'll pretend that nothing out of the ordinary has happened, she thought, looking out the window. Now, for the first time, she noticed that they were on a lonely road. I must act normally, persuade him to drive to a busier part of town.

"What is it? What's wrong?" she asked.

"The phone call."

"Sue's? My friend's?"

"Christ, no! The murder you overheard."

"What about it? I've told you all I know. Listen, let's just get out of here—go downtown. They'll be expecting us." She started to slide back to her side of the car, but he grabbed her by the arm and pulled her along after him as he opened the door and got out.

"Hey, what are you doing?" She tried unsuccessfully to jerk free of his grip as he got back into the car and pulled her into the driver's seat.

"You drive," he ordered.

Her brain seemed to be working in slow motion. She wanted to ask questions, unravel her thoughts, but then, in a flash of horror, she saw he was holding a knife, a kitchen knife, and her head cleared immediately. She took a sharp breath and felt her insides go slack like soft gelatin. But her mind exploded with questions. How had this happened? How was it that he had arrived at the door instead of Bill Graham?

"How did you know Lieutenant Graham was coming over this evening?"

He hesitated a moment, then said, "I called your work yesterday, pretending to be a policeman. Whoever I talked to assumed I was Graham. They told me about your husband—your ex-husband—and the blind date you had this evening, but it was just chance that I caught you at home. And you never questioned who I was. I just followed along with your suggestion to leave the house."

"And Sue was right," Lora said with a sinking feeling. "You killed L.J.—Laura—didn't you? Thinking it was me."

He didn't answer her question. "Drive."

"How did you make such a mistake?" She could hear a hysterical accusation in her voice and knew she must get hold of herself.

He reached above her, pulled a UACA directory from behind the visor and tossed it onto the dashboard. "She had the misfortune of being the only Laura in the Claims Department. And it didn't occur to me to watch out for a different way of spelling. Now, cut out this crap and drive."

"Where to?" she asked weakly.

"I don't know, but just away from the city."

She flirted with possibilities. Drive up to a police station? He would notice if she started back toward town. Run off the road? That would probably kill her and leave him free.

"I want you to think of someplace we can go, someplace to give me some time to think," he told her.

After a moment she said, "There's a company recreational area on a lake near here. It's private, probably not being used, at least until tomorrow. I have a card to get in the gate."

With her peripheral vision, she saw him shake his head. "I can't risk you showing a card to someone."

"No, no," she explained. "There's no one there. You just put a card in a gate opener." Maybe if they got there, she could escape across the lake. The thought of swimming across that expanse—frightened her in a different way—all that black water surrounding her, threatening to engulf her. But if it were the only way, she could do it.

"Do you have the card?"

"In my purse."

He reached down to the floorboard and felt around. It was there. He pulled it up and slung it onto the seat between them. "Go there," he said, "to the recreational area. And I don't want you to go too fast or too slow. I don't want you to attract any attention, you understand? Don't get any crazy ideas."

"The police—they know all about you. They'll start looking for me when they come to pick me up and I'm not there." She realized they wouldn't know what kind of car she was in. "They're probably already looking. You can't get away with it, you know." She didn't dare go so far as to put *it* into words. Saying it might make it more real, might make it come true. Shut up, Lora, she told herself. Do you want to push him beyond whatever limit he has, with your yammering? But should she be assertive or passive? God, she thought, this was the same sort of dilemma women were fighting everywhere, for every kind of reason.

She tried to concentrate on the road, following the two-lane strip of blacktop into the countryside. They had left the suburbs of Dallas far behind, and now the sky was completely dark. The clapboard houses of people who wanted to raise a few animals or have a truck farm dotted the landscape at approximately quarter-mile intervals, each with its mercury-vapor light illuminating the yard, forming pools of what looked like safety to Lora.

Would he really kill her? she wondered. Should she just be passive and hope that he wouldn't? Would that be best? Then she remembered reading about some women in a beauty shop in Arizona who simply lay down on the floor and waited to be murdered. And the nurses in Chicago who one by one were executed. And there was L.J. Better to do something than just passively wait to die. But what to do? She was a claims representative with no skills particularly suited for survival.

In order to take things into her own hands, to take control away from him, she would have to catch this man off guard. His knife was too handy for carelessness on her part, so she watched him surreptitiously, waiting till he became forgetful of it, just for a moment. When that happened, she might, just might, have a chance to reach one of those oases of light. If the timing was perfect.

They passed a small house, all dark except for the yard light. She glanced at him—Tony, that's what Bill had said his name was—but he met her glance almost as if he had anticipated it. And the look he gave her helped crystallize her thoughts. It was cold, hateful. But that electricity. What was it? What had happened between them? She shuddered, still aware of the sensitivity of her lips from the pressure of his kiss. But he was a violent man, she knew that, and he no doubt meant to kill her; it was just a matter of when. She must, then, interfere with his idea of her destiny.

Another house with a fence around it slid by, rejected. Unsuitable for her purpose—a purpose that had given her new fortitude, mentally, at least. Her stomach still felt weak. She scrutinized the countryside with growing calmness and a critical eye as she waited for the right moment. It finally arrived.

The shingled house was a fuzzy green color in the arc of light bathing the yard and outbuildings. No fence, no obstructions in the yard. There were lights on inside.

She glanced at Tony. He was looking away momentarily.

She swerved abruptly, braking simultaneously, throwing the car into a skid and Tony hard against the right door and forward at the same time. She braced herself to stay behind the wheel just long enough, then threw open the door and rolled out.

''What in—'' he exclaimed before he realized what she was doing.

Oh, God. She didn't know how it would hurt. Television stunt people made it look so easy, taking tremendous falls and walking away without a hair out of place, but she was sliding along the gravel-impacted road, peeling the skin off her forearms, loose gravel digging into her abdomen. The road acted like a grater on her clothes, shredding them, leaving her exposed to the sandpaper of the road's surface for the moment before she reached the blessed softness of the highway's shoulder. She struggled to her feet, now in her stockings—her shoes lost in the road—but when she tried to put her right foot on the ground, the right ankle wouldn't support her without a sharp pain drilling into her. Somewhere, muffled by the shock of her pain, she heard the civilized sound of a barking dog, not realizing how ominous it was.

She glanced back and saw that the car had regained a steady path after bumping through the drainage ditch and back onto the road. She had to move, couldn't just stand there waiting for the burning agony to subside.

"He was too quick," she cried aloud, limping toward the house, the agony of her ankle stabbing through her. "Help," she shouted. "Please help me!" But no one seemed to be around. Except the dog. She saw the scene before her unfolding as if in a movie, with tendrils of pain twisting her perception.

Her planning had been defective. Every farm had a watchdog, and this one came lunging toward her from around the corner of the house, its eyes like black pits in the surreal light, its mouth pulled back in a cruel grin. It reached her just then, throwing its full weight against her. A big dog, not a Doberman, but with that same sinewy body, as heavy as she. She threw her arms out, flailing in the air, trying to hit it as she lost her balance and fell heavily on one knee. She made contact, a dull thud with her fist against the dog's head, but the blow didn't faze the animal. The dog sank its teeth into her, its slobbering mouth fitting easily around her arm. The pain shot through her in searing pricks. She could smell the heavy odor of its body as she struck out at it again with her free arm, struggling to her feet. Half running, the best she could manage with her bad ankle, she tried to get away, kicking at the animal, trying to throw it off.

Why didn't the people look outside? There was a goddamn war going on in their front yard and no one had even come to the window. She dragged herself against the weight of the dog, which had let go of her arm and was now tearing into her ankle. It scrambled along with her.

"Help!" she yelled at the top of her lungs, feeling it

would be her last chance to be heard before the dog ripped her apart.

The car was coming toward her, across the yard, its headlights off. Tony came leaping out, grabbed her by the arm and tried to drag her back to the car, but the dog's attention was drawn to the new intruder and it tore into him just as it had into her. While Tony grappled with it, Lora took the chance to run. Tony was between her and the car, and she was certain by now that no one in the house was going to help, if anyone were home, so she hobbled on her painful ankle as fast as she could toward a barn at the back of the house. Maybe she could hide inside it until someone came home. She had to get *somewhere*, had to hide, had to rest a moment. In the back of her consciousness she became aware that the sounds from the dog had stopped, meaning Tony was probably after her again. In answer to her thought, she heard the purr of the car as it started down the driveway toward the barn.

She unlatched the barn door and pulled it back just enough to slip in. But it seemed impossible. She was facing a wall of hay. She glanced around and saw the car coming down the driveway. Looking up, she could see the top of the bales over her head. Quickly, clenching her teeth in determination, she grabbed hold of the twine around one bale, dug her good foot into the side of the next-to-lowest bale, and hoisted herself up with a nimbleness she hadn't known she still possessed. She winced as the twine cut into her already pain-wracked hands. Her ankle throbbed, but adrenaline surged through her, forcing her onward, giving her the strength to haul herself up farther. Hand over hand, she climbed. She reached the top and stopped a moment to rest, gasping for breath, then crawled across, the hay offending the rawness of her shins.

She would hide in here somewhere; there had to be a place. She came to a ladder against the side of the barn, paused momentarily, then decided not to climb it. She didn't want to get trapped in a loft.

The pungent hay filled the front half of the barn, wall to wall, but the back half seemed to be more or less empty. She clambered down off the bales clumsily, favoring one foot. The barn was dark, with just a haze of light coming in above the hay through the door to the outside. As she blindly groped along the side wall of the building, her hand touched an implement of some kind. She slid her fingers down the handle to where wood was attached to metal, then splayed into deadly fingers. A pitchfork. A weapon. Feeling her way back along the wall, she came to the hay again and moved her hands along the prickly surfaces till she found a niche to hide in, where several bales had been removed.

She would have given anything to have known where Tony was now. But she just had to wait, hoping to hear some sound as a clue to his whereabouts. She squatted, panting, her legs cramped, as she tried to get ready for the next onslaught, which she knew was coming. She leaned her head back against the hay and tried to calm herself. The waiting was terrible; she felt her heart was going to burst out of her.

45

Bill Graham pulled up in front of Lora's house. He had had a little trouble finding it, but there was still plenty of time to get downtown. He realized his heart was beating a little faster, just anticipating seeing her, even for a professional reason.

He went to the door eagerly and knocked once, twice, but no one answered. He walked around the house to see if there was any way inside, but everything was locked up. He couldn't understand where she could be, unless the two of them had gotten their signals crossed and she hadn't understood he would pick her up. That didn't seem likely, though. Besides, a car was in the driveway and he doubted if she had two, being single. Maybe a friend had driven her down.

The next door neighbor was putting luggage in his car, the dome light illuminating him. A woman came out of their house just then, carrying several bags, with a young child racing along behind her chattering a blue streak. An older child, a boy, was standing in the doorway. Bill could see his outline against the lights in the house.

"Have you seen Mrs. Montgomery?" he asked all of them.

"Yes, she was there just a little while ago," the woman volunteered, stopping on her way to the car. "I was over, but she was leaving. By the way, I'm Helen Myers."

Bill frowned. "Did she mention where she was going?" The next door neighbor pulled himself out of his car to listen.

"No, but I think she must have had a date, since there was a nice-looking young man with her."

Just then a car pulled up in front and a man got out in a hurry and went up to Lora's house.

Bill's hand went inside his coat, where his shoulder holster lay, and he moved quickly to the porch, coming up behind the man. "Police. You want to tell me who you are?"

The man turned, startled. "God, you scared me to death. Martin Montgomery. This is my ex-wife's house."

Bill, seeing that the man wasn't Longoria, took out his I.D. "These people say she left a while ago with some man. Do you have any idea who that might have been?"

"Could it have been this guy who's out to get her? From New York?"

Bill frowned. "She was supposed to be meeting him at the Hyatt. I was going to drive her down."

"She told me she was meeting him, but she didn't tell me how she was getting there. Listen, this is kind of complicated, but let me tell you why I came out here." He told Bill his story.

"Christ. That's what I'm worried about. Let me check something out with these people." He fumbled in his pocket for the picture of Tony as he walked back to where the Myerses were watching. Martin followed. "Was this the guy she was with?" he asked Helen Myers.

She took it and held it toward the light in the car.

"I'm sure it is. He's younger here, but you don't forget a face like that." She handed it back to Bill.

"Can you tell me what kind of a car they left in?" he asked Helen.

"I'm sorry, I can't. Just that it was maroon. I'm not much good with cars."

The boy, who had come out of the house to see what was going on, piped up. "I saw it. It was a 1982 Toronado."

"Good boy! You didn't happen to notice the license number, too?"

The boy shook his head.

"Well, you've been a big help." He turned to the man. "One more thing. May I use your phone?"

They all went in with him, including Martin, and waited while he called the Dallas police. Bill talked to the detective in charge, telling him what had happened. They would get out an APB on the vehicle, such as the description was. A man and woman in a maroon Toronado—a needle in a haystack in Dallas. Or Texas. How many minutes had they been gone?

46

Carl Moore looked in the mirror and brushed his hair one more time. He was filled with a mixture of anticipation and dread. He hated blind dates. For that matter, he hated dates.

He was a writer. And this was undoubtedly the craziest thing he had ever done, because he had just outright lied to that woman on the phone. Told her his name was Thad Morrow. Well, it was, sort of, he guessed. That was one of his pseudonyms, the one for his paperback adventure series. He was also Autumn Winfield, for the bodice rippers, and Jonathan Day, for the westerns.

And it was definitely a Thad Morrow type or one of his characters who had made the date. Carl Moore wouldn't have done it; he was a retiring sort of fellow who occasionally steeled himself to do a speaking engagement such as he was doing in Dallas this weekend at a writer's conference. The whole thing had been coincidental—about getting hold of a claims person in Dallas. But why hadn't he told her his real name? The anonymity of the telephone, he guessed. The same thing that gave pre-teenagers so much courage on the phone. It was going to be embarrassing to have to confess. And how would he get his claim processed without confessing? He'd probably just write the tape deck off.

He looked in the mirror again, and what he saw didn't please him. He was average sized, but frumpy looking. His skin was sallow from his indoor life, and his hair had a tendency to spring out in its own way, no matter how he coaxed it to do otherwise. Why wouldn't his tie hang straight? He twisted it. She would surely be disappointed. Of course, what did he know about her? A nice voice doesn't a beauty make. And how exciting could her life be, a claims person?

Well, he thought, I'll just have to put this whole thing down as grist for the creative mill. Actually, he was tickled by his own discomfiture. He closed his eyes and let his imagination play. For that was one thing Carl Moore had going for him: a lot of imagination. What would happen if I made dates this way over the phone all the time? What if it was a scam of some sort? But what sort? he wondered. What would happen if . . . ?

He took one last look, then turned out the lamp and went to the door of his room. It was time to go down to meet her in the lobby. He hoped he wouldn't be too surprised.

47

"Put out an APB on a maroon-colored Toronado, male and female occupants. Female, late thirties, medium-length brown hair. Male, late twenties, dark curly hair, six feet, dangerous. Woman is a hostage."

Bart's hand was shaking by the time he finished the transmission. That was his goddamn car, he was sure of it. That curly-headed six-foot male was his Joe Thomas. Jeez, what a predicament. He needed to give them the license number, but he sure as hell hated to explain how he got tangled up with the guy.

"Tell me about this," he said to the sergeant.

"Some New York shithead down here to kill a witness or something like that. I don't know. But if she's here, how's she a witness? I think there's a report about the punk floating around here. Let me see."

The picture the sergeant dredged up with the report was a young Joe Thomas, a.k.a. Tony Longoria.

"You okay?" he asked Bart.

"Yeah, except the shithead has my car. That's my maroon Toronado."

"No shit? Stolen?"

"I wish." He sighed heavily, thinking maybe that's what he should have reported, but the notion of lying about it interfered with his code of behavior. "I loaned it to him. Christ, I didn't know he was a felon."

Lonnie was always chiding him about his willingness to accept people just as they were, good and bad. And he was ready to let Joe, or whatever his name was, just be. He guessed he should have been more suspicious of the guy's willingness to stay with him in the face of his obvious antagonism toward gays.

He thought back to how incredulous Joe, this Tony, had acted when they pulled up at headquarters this afternoon.

"You're a cop?"

"Dispatcher. This is where you'll pick me up. Okay?"

"Yeah, sure," he had said, still big-eyed. Now Bart understood why. Well, his eyes were going to get even bigger, according to this report, when he kept an appointment he had at the Hyatt.

When Bart finished the report, he pushed it back across the counter to the sergeant, then took a pen from his pocket and wrote his license-plate number on a note pad on the desktop. "Give that to the lieutenant. Tell him I'm getting coffee, then I'll be in to talk to him."

48

Goddamn it to hell, Tony thought. He had slit the dog's throat, but not before it had almost made mincemeat of his arm. He stopped the car before the barn door and saw her disappear over the top of the wall of hay that was exposed in the narrow opening by his headlights. He got out quickly and went over, planning to pursue her, but thinking better of it. She would just run out the other end of the barn. He needed to smoke her out, he thought, meaning it figuratively, but immediately seeing an advantage to the real thing. He reached in his pocket for his disposable lighter and held it up to a piece of the hay. It glowed red while he continued to hold his lighter against it until other bits caught. His eyes widened as he gazed raptly at the growing fire before him, until its heat began to drive him back.

Shaking his head as if to clear it, he moved away and decided to circle the barn to see what avenues of escape Lora would have. If he narrowed her route to one, he could scoop her up as she fled the fire. The idea of leaving her inside, letting her asphyxiate or burn to death, didn't fit his plan, because he wanted her alive, at least for a while.

The sight of her waiting there for him at her house—well, Lieutenant Graham, really—had startled him because he had recognized her from when he'd gone to the personnel office at UACA—and, God, she looked so ripe, her whole body just begging for him to savor it—he wanted her, to feel her body under his, to have a taste of her. Then he would do the other.

The corner of his mouth twitched and he rubbed it to make it stop. He had to be tough, quit thinking about her like that. The touching, that could come later, when they got someplace safe.

For now he would make sure there was only one way out.

49

Finally, she heard a sound. Her head jerked up alertly, but it took her a moment to realize what it was. The smell confirmed it—he had set the year-old hay on fire. It would take little time for a small blaze to be a sweeping inferno; the barn itself, oak, dry-weathered from the Texas sun, would catch like tinder. She quickly climbed down the bales, rushing headlong toward the back of the barn, to the doors she hoped might be there, panic seizing her, holding her in a tight grip. Already she could hear the crackling of the fire as it sent its tentacles deeper into the barn. She fell over something lying in the middle of the floor, staggered up and stumbled on until she threw herself blindly against the doors. But they didn't budge. She tried again, fear grabbing her by the throat and choking her, but the doors were firmly braced from the outside.

The sweet smoke was beginning to permeate the air, but it was rising first to fill and drift through the top of the tall barn. As the fire grew, though, it would begin to press downward, trapping her, filling her lungs. Desperately she felt along the back wall, then came to the corner and began her search along the east wall. She moved frantically, groping for another way out, a way to evade the suffocating smoke. Her eyes were beginning to water and she blinked to evade the stinging fumes. She came to a door and turned the handle. Begrudgingly the door opened and Lora pushed through, jamming it shut behind her. She paused for a breath, taking it in deeply to clear her lungs, and noticed a different smell, a musty, sickening stench.

With dismay she realized she still wasn't free. What she had hoped was a way out was just a door into another room. She was at the side of the barn, she knew that, but was still trapped inside. And the new smell was causing her mouth to draw up inside as if she were going to be sick.

She reached out in the pitch-dark, grappling for anything to give her a sense of place. She took a step and her foot sank into something squishy, oozing up between her toes. She began to retch, her throat constricting rhythmically, but she couldn't afford to give in to sickness. Instead, she forced herself to continue her search. She reached out, touching something, then jerked back in reflexive terror of the unknown as the object set up a squawk. A chicken. She was in a chicken coop. She could see a window, vaguely, its lighter rectangle visible in front of her. She felt her way to it, arms stretched out before her, bare feet moving through the slime on the floor. She imagined hookworms crawling up her legs. The window was stuck fast or nailed shut. She couldn't even find a latch. She grabbed the roost the chickens were squatting on and tried to dislodge it to use as a tool. The hens came at her, flapping and squawking, cackling in criticism, disoriented by this strange intrusion in the night. She flailed at them with her hands, trying to keep them away.

The smoke was beginning to seep in now. She could feel it contaminating the air, mingling with the overpowering smell of the chicken debris. Desperately she dropped to her hands and knees in the muck, which was partly dry and decayed, partly fresh and wet, looking for something with which to break the window, her hands searching through the putrid-smelling chicken droppings. Now her eyes were at a lower level than before and she became aware of another lighter area on the outside wall—the opening the chickens came through. Would she fit? Oh, dear God, I have to, I have to get out of here, she told herself. She stuck her head through and oozed her body out, twisting and turning, sucking her breath in, scraping her hips through, thinking how her clothes were a hindrance, pulling with her arms, struggling and managing to get out and down the little ramp the chickens used.

The barnyard was well-lighted now from the fire, which was beginning to engulf the entire front of the building. The heat was building; already perspiring, she could now feel the sweat dripping down her sides. On her face it was difficult to tell the tears from the sweat. She limped to the chicken-yard gate and opened it cautiously, stepped through and went to the front corner of the barn, and looked cautiously around. No sign of Tony. The car stood where she could see it, just in front of the blazing barn.

The fire lighted the yard, the roar harsh in the night. Soon, she knew someone would come. She could just wait here. A car on the road would see it, report it. The people would come home. A neighbor, still up, would see it. It was just a matter of waiting.

But Tony was nowhere in sight. And the driver's door of the car, her own familiar car, stood open, inviting her in—a Circe, irresistible.

Without another moment of hesitation, she half ran, half staggered toward the car. She saw a movement out of the corner of her eye and knew without looking who was there. He was coming around the other side of the barn. She turned, doubling back, heading for a field. She crawled over a board fence, dropped down and began to run, her gait lopsided, clumsy. The winter stubble of grass awaiting spring cut into her feet belligerently. Her breathing came in sharp gasps now, but she had to keep going. She knew she was no match for a man running, so she didn't dare even look around to see how close he was. She was aware suddenly of the breeze tickling the hair on her arm, cool to her skin, as on so many other spring evenings, but now she seemed in some primordial world a million miles from nowhere, with no resources but her own.

His hand grabbed her upper arm, stopping her abruptly, swinging her down to the ground. She kicked out randomly, screaming, a trapped animal reacting to capture. Then the fight went out of her and he dragged her up by both arms, pulling her, her own pain forcing her to obey as he wrenched her arms almost to the breaking point.

At the fence he bullied her over, still twisting her arm, then he followed. When they reached the car, he opened its trunk, and, with what felt like her last effort, she asked, "What are you doing?" even though the answer was obvious.

50

"Don't put me in there. I promise I won't try to get away or yell or anything." Her breathing became shallow just thinking about being trapped in the trunk, locked in.

He was searching the contents with one hand. There was a bungee cord and a pile of rags. Not much else. He shoved her, urging her inside, but she balked. "Get in," he ordered.

She crawled over the back of the trunk, but not fast enough to suit him, so he prodded her with the point of a knife. Once she was inside, he forced her onto her stomach, then took the stretchy cord and wrapped it around her wrists twice, hooking it somewhere.

She was struggling, sobbing again, panicking. She threw her neck back and held her mouth open, hyperventilating, trying to drink in the air to sustain herself. He grabbed a handful of her hair and turned her head sideways, then stuffed a dirty rag in her mouth. She gagged, struggling not to vomit. The muscles in her throat started reflexively reversing, trying to cast out the wad of cloth.

Then the trunk lid slammed, isolating her in a cocoon of fear.

From somewhere in her past she dragged out a mantra, a phrase tailored just for her by a yogi from another time and place, and she began to recite it. She had learned it during a yoga class she had taken in the early seventies, when yoga was in vogue. Martin had thought she was silly, but she'd enjoyed it, something a little different from her ordinary existence. The teacher had taken them all to meet a guru. She had been sent alone into a darkened room, in a stripped-down house where some hippies lived. A bearded man in a white robe, sitting in the lotus position, had whispered a mantra to her. It was her very own, not to share with anyone, he had said. The discipline of meditation had gradually slipped away from her and she'd forgotten the mantra over the years, but now it came back.

She recited it, over and over again, trying to concentrate on the feeling of the words in her head, the shapes of each letter, molding them, hypnotizing herself.

Then her mind rebelled, flirting with what was happening to her. She heard the door slam, and the car began to move.

The words. Say the words.

I am dying, she thought. I can't get enough air. Her nostrils flared, trying to suck in more.

The words. Say the words. Concentrate on them. The shapes.

The car swerved, then stopped.

Her curiosity about what he was doing overcame her overwhelming preoccupation with her predicament for a moment. Where are we? she wondered.

The sounds became familiar, and she realized he'd stopped for gas. She vaguely remembered a convenience store at the corner where they turned to go to the lake. She could smell the heady aroma of gasoline, intoxicating her senses.

Maybe after he gets gas he'll let me out, to show him the way to the lake, she thought. He won't know where to go without me.

Concentrate on the mantra. The words were nonsense to her, their repetition everything, all she had. It wouldn't take much longer now, and he would let her out—to show him the way. Yes, he will do that. He needs me to get him to a safe place.

She kept trying to keep the mantra in her head, saying the words monotonously, concentrating on them. Somewhere in the distance she heard two loud reports, then, moments later, footsteps, insistent, hurried. Someone got into a car. She made sounds, muffled through the rag. Maybe someone would hear. An engine turned over and died. Again.

Why didn't Tony come? She so desperately wanted him to let her out of here.

A car door slammed, and she made muffled sounds again.

She heard footsteps coming to her car. Was it someone from the car that wouldn't start? Or was it Tony? Probably—there had been plenty of time for him to return, so she shut up and went back to her mantra. She couldn't take the chance of enraging him, pushing him into killing her. The longer she stayed alive, the more of a chance she might have.

Soon he'll let me out. He'll need me to show him the way to the lake, she convinced herself again. I still have some importance to him.

Knowing that she would soon be free of the trunk gave her a momentary sense of elation. She would make it now. The engine was alive. They were pulling out in a hurry; her body was thrown back against the back of the trunk. Down the road a little he would surely let her out. It wouldn't take long now. And she would lead him to the lake, then make a break for it across the water.

But something was wrong. He wasn't stopping. He was going faster. He couldn't have forgotten her, so what had happened? Was this to be it? she thought, tears of desperation filling her eyes. He will leave me here to suffocate and die. Well, of course, that's what he wanted, and he was obviously having trouble just killing her. This would be the easy way out for him. Panic began to rise in her again. She struggled to get the rag out of her mouth, but just succeeded in wedging it in farther. It gagged her, threatening to asphyxiate her.

51

Deputy Sheriff Wylie was sitting in his car on a side road, drinking coffee, black, from a thermos, when he saw the car go by. It was nothing unusual, not traveling at a high rate of speed or anything. But he had just heard the bulletin advising the police to be on the lookout for that particular car model and color. There was a woman missing. He knew the model pretty well because it was what the wife drove. He got to drive an old pickup. Wouldn't have it any other way. But his wife didn't want to be caught dead in his fishing truck.

He screwed the lid on the thermos and started the car, pulling in behind the other car at about a quarter-mile distance.

He picked up the radio, gave Betty, the dispatcher, his

whereabouts, then gave his full attention to following the lights in the isolated darkness. He began to close the distance, so he could get a look at the license number. He wasn't running with his cruiser lights on, but as he drew closer, the other car sped up.

The deputy called in for assistance, then accelerated and turned on his cherry top. It was as if he had activated a turbo boost on the other car by remote control. It took off in a spray of fine gravel, careening around the next intersection, fishtailing as it took the corner. By the time Wylie made the corner, the other driver had turned out his lights and was driving blind through the dark.

Must know these roads pretty well, by howdy, Wylie thought. Bigod, he'd better, cause it's black as pitch out here.

He radioed in again, telling his location, then began to scan the road ahead for some sign of the car. And he found it.

52

The car had changed direction; it was going back the way they had come. But why? Lora didn't understand.

Something happened back there, she thought briefly, just as the vehicle surged forward, throwing her body violently backward. It took a corner, spinning her into the side of the trunk, wrenching her head up, then slamming it down. She tried to hold her neck rigid to resist the relentless depredations on her head, but then the car jolted in a new direction. She could no longer anticipate what would happen next. Her physical strength was sapped; there were no new resources to call upon. She would have screamed if she could have, because her whole body was screaming. But the only sound she could make was muffled and no relief to her pain.

The last thing she heard was the squeal of the brakes. Then she was toppling over, unable to brace herself, her bruised body absorbing the brutal force of a wreck. The blackness around her became complete as she lost consciousness.

53

A departing siren is what first sank through to her unconscious and began to pull her back. Then she heard voices.

Her position had changed. She was disoriented and not sure she wanted to awaken, because it seemed as if her whole body was aflame with pain. But she had no choice; consciousness came unbidden.

The voices drew nearer, and she began to make what sounds she could manage, surprised that she *could* still manage because the way her body felt, she should be dead by now.

"Let's check through the car—see if there's any sign of the woman."

The woman. Could they mean her? She made as loud a noise as possible.

"D'you hear somethin'?" a deep voice said.

"Yeah. Sounds like it's coming from the trunk," came the reply, then loudly: "Hey, you guys, come over here and help us get this trunk open."

Lora was kicking the inside of the trunk now.

"We're gonna get you outta there—hold on," a voice said.

"See if the keys are still in the ignition."

A pause, then: "Yeah, here they are."

She heard the key being inserted. "Okay, now, her weight's gonna be on the lid, so let's all lower it slowly. Ray, you get on that side. Good. Okay, here we go."

And then blessed fresh air hit her face.

"Get a flashlight over here," one of the men commanded.

The beam of a flashlight hit her in the face, and almost simultaneously someone—some saint—pulled the rag out of her mouth.

She began to sob with relief, managing to work in a heartfelt and broken "Thank you." They seemed to be waiting, not knowing how to move her, so after she got control of her voice, she said, "My wrists—could you unhook the strap? I—I think I'm okay." She heard herself say the words, though not really believing them since every square inch of her body felt as if it had been tortured in a unique way. There were the stinging places and the throbbing ones, the dull and the sharp. But she was alive, and that's all that really mattered.

One of the men unfastened her wrists, and she tentatively moved, not sure what hurt the most.

"Can you move everything?" someone asked.

"Yes, I think so. Just help me out." She seemed still to be in one piece, even though the whole front of her body felt abraded. She pulled herself up, with two of the men helping her crawl out of the trunk, wincing as they took hold of her raw flesh. One supported her as she weakly pulled herself upright. Her ankle was painful and she began to tremble all over. She felt as if she might throw up.

"We'll take you over to the sheriff's car." The man made a move to step away, releasing his grip, and she almost sank. Quickly, he took hold of her again. "Here," he said. "You need some assistance. Joe, take ahold of her other arm." The three of them moved haltingly to the sheriff's car, and she was feeling steadier by the time they got there. At least the nausea was gone.

"Tell us what happened," one of the men who had been supporting her said when they had settled her in the backseat.

"What—What happened to the man who was driving?" she asked, her voice tremulous, sounding faraway, like someone else's voice.

"Dead," one said. "He was thrown from the car. They've taken his body away already."

One of the men noticed her shudder and said, "Get a blanket out of the trunk, will you, Joe?" Then he asked her: "How'd you end up in that trunk?"

"It's a long story. That man came to Dallas to kill me, but I didn't know he was the one at first. He—He kidnapped me, then he put me in—" She passed her hands over her face, remembering those first minutes in the trunk. "He put me in there. I'm lucky you found me." She leaned her head back against the seat and closed her eyes.

"It wasn't luck. We were looking for your car. The Dallas police set us on it. And Deputy Wylie"—a man standing adjacent to the car touched his hat—"he saw the car go by."

"Yes, m'am, I saw the car go by, and when I started to follow, the driver began acting suspiciously."

Suspiciously, that was a good word for it, thought Lora. Why did he change his mind about going to the lake? It was a fateful decision, for whatever reason. Now she was still alive and safe and he was dead. She heaved a sigh; the ordeal was over.

Well, not quite. Joe slammed the trunk down and she grimaced as it jarred the backseat. The thoughtful sheriff—she guessed he was the sheriff—tucked the blanket around her legs when Joe handed it to him, then went around to the driver's seat.

Either from fatigue or mild shock, Lora was in an altered state of consciousness. Occasionally, her fog would lift, her head would seem to clear, and it felt as if she'd just awakened. Operating from this new sense of reality, she'd watch the countryside speed by outside the cocoon of the sheriff's car until, distressingly, a new cloud would descend, nullifying what she had just been experiencing.

As they pulled away from the scene of the wreck, she insisted that she didn't need hospitalization. But the sheriff, Wade Tomlin, had firmly countered that he wanted her looked at. She was too tired to resist the pressure brought to bear by his resemblance to her father, making him someone to reckon with.

Her father had ruled the house, hadn't allowed her to date till she was sixteen, hadn't put up with any adolescent nonsense. And for some reason Lora hadn't rebelled. What was it in her makeup that kept her towing the line? Sometimes she thought sadly that she was still being that same good girl. Who was it for, after all? That thought didn't occur to her now, facing the law officer, but the force of her father was still at work.

54

The clerk was dead behind the counter, slumped against the wall. The open, staring eyes on the lolling head, were the first thing Tony saw as he regained consciousness. He stood up, putting his hand to his head and coming away with a palmful of blood where a bullet had grazed it, knocking him down, his head coming brutally into contact with the tile-covered concrete floor. The sight of it made him feel weak in the chest, and he closed his eyes momentarily and grabbed for the counter. The feeling passed and he glanced around, seeing what was presumably the door to the back room and maybe a restroom where he could wipe the blood away. In the small, dirty restroom he washed his hands, then dampened a length of stiff paper towels and tried to wash the wound on his head. Finally he leaned over and splashed water on his hair, using the paper towel to wipe it. His blood, thinned by the water, covered the sink and washed down the drain. He didn't seem to be making much progress, but he had to get on the move before someone came, so he stopped and took a wad of toilet paper, which was softer, and just pressed it against his head to staunch the flow. He knew a scalp wound could bleed profusely without being too serious.

He left the washroom, and without a glance at the dead clerk, went to the front door. A look outside made him feel he'd lived two lives in one night, and the second one was becoming more complicated by the minute because the Toronado was gone. A beat-up old blue Skylark, which presumably had been the stickup man's car, was still there. If the keys weren't there . . .

He'd been glad when he reached the convenience store that there were few customers. Just one guy. He should have looked more closely before he went bumbling in, but he'd been absorbed in his own problems. Too late, he saw that the punk was holding a gun on the clerk.

The kid, startled by Tony's entrance, had turned and . . . as the impact of the shot blew Tony off his feet, he hit his head and lost consciousness. He never heard another shot.

The keys were in the Skylark. He got in before noticing something else that might come in handy. There was a gun, a Saturday Night Special, lying on the seat. Tony noted it, but didn't have time to examine it. He had to get out of there before another customer came along.

The engine didn't turn over on the first try, nor on the second. He sat there a moment, then tried again. This time, with a sick grinding, it started. Tony drank a gulp of air, feeling he could start breathing again.

He went back the way they had come, wondering briefly where in the hell Lora was by now.

55

The hospital was a small community facility on the outskirts of Dallas where the nurses still had time to be solicitous. After Lora was checked over, given a tetanus shot for the dog bites, and her ankle X-rayed to make sure there were no hairline fractures, one of the nurses, a tiny thing rippling with energy, helped her clean up.

"Is there anyone I can call to bring you some clean clothes?"

"Yes, my ex-husband. He has a key to my house." She thought briefly about the last time he'd used that key, for his and Serena's tryst. If he hadn't gone there, then Serena would have been somewhere else, would have never been attacked. Tears began to pour out of her eyes for no immediate reason.

"You poor thing," the nurse said, wrapping her arms around Lora. "Just have a good cry. You've had a terrible time of it."

"But I don't need to cry now," Lora babbled.

"Sure you do," the nurse consoled, patting Lora's back, one of the few parts of her that was relatively free of abrasions. They stood there a few minutes like that, the nurse reassuring Lora, until Lora sniffed back her tears and pulled away. "Thanks," she said, drawing her index finger under her nose. "I guess I did need that."

"You okay now?"

Lora nodded, smiling weakly. "I think so."

"Let me have your ex's number."

Lora gave it to her, but also explained how he might be with Serena and where he might be reached.

"I'll be back to look in on you soon."

Lora limped to the bathroom to look at herself in a mirror. Her face was bruised, particularly on the side that had rested on the floor of the trunk. She examined the mark on her neck and shook her head; she looked like a prize fighter. She held up the hospital gown and peered down at the abrasions appearing along the whole front of her body, even her legs, where she had slid along the asphalt road. Her body felt as if it were on fire, even though they had given her a painkiller.

Her feet and ankle harbored the deepest pain, but fortunately the bones weren't broken and the muscles were just strained. She limped back to the bed, trying to miss the scratches and abrasions on the soles of her feet. Laying back on the bed carefully, she pulled her legs up, wincing as she bent them. When she was settled, she sighed deeply, hating to have too much time to examine her feelings about Tony. Would she have felt that magnetism if she had known who he was from the start? If she had known he wasn't Bill Graham? She didn't want to think it was pure, unadulterated lust, and yet she had to admit that Tony had exuded a raw sexuality.

Her thoughts were interrupted by a tap on the door, and after a moment the sheriff, a deeply-tanned, stocky man with deep wrinkles furrowing his neck, stuck his head in. "Thought I'd check in on you." He took his hat off, revealing a baby-smooth white band across his forehead, where the Texas sun seldom reached.

"Well, I think I'm going to make it," Lora said. "I'm sore, but in one piece."

"That fella killed the convenience store operator where you stopped."

Lora's eyes widened. "Oh, no. How terrible." She looked down at her hands and said, "It's hard to believe, even after everything that's happened." Murders were something for the television news or the newspaper, not real life. Despite her recent brush with death, to her mind murderers didn't come into contact with ordinary people.

The sheriff nodded. "We just found out. One of my men went over there and found the man. The fellow who kidnapped you—what was his name?"

"It was Tony—Tony something-or-other." She closed her eyes, trying to remember his last name, but couldn't. "He told me he was a policeman," she said, then amended it: "Well, actually, I was expecting a policeman and I just assumed—"

"Oh? He didn't have a lick of identification on him." He had gotten out a notebook and was making notes. "Now you told us he was trying to kill you—you want to tell me more about it?"

"I overheard him kill someone."

He frowned. "Overheard?"

"I'm an insurance claims representative. A woman called me, and while she was talking to me, he came in and started beating her up. I didn't know he had killed her, I found that out later, but she must have left my number there and he knew I had heard what happened. So he came to Dallas looking for me."

"Apparently something happened in there to make him kill that clerk," he said, and then waited, as if she would come up with an explanation.

She closed her eyes, bringing it all back. "I don't know. But he set a fire at a barn not too far from there."

The sheriff's left eyebrow crooked upward. "Jess Parks' place. It's a real mess. Why'd he wanna go and do that?"

"I was in there. I had jumped out of the car and tried to get to the house, but no one was home. Then I ran into the barn."

The nurse reappeared just then. "Oh, I'm sorry," she said, "didn't mean to interrupt anything."

"That's okay, we're about finished," the sheriff told her. He asked her a few more questions, then put his notebook and pad back in his shirt pocket, replaced his hat, and said, "Now, you take care; you've had a rough time and I imagine you'll be questioned lots more."

"She did have a rough time," the nurse agreed. She pulled the top sheet gently out from under Lora and helped her get under it. "You just relax now; that painkiller will help you get some sleep, and when you wake up, they'll probably let you go home." She left, turning out the light as she went.

Lora lay in the semidark room, trying to focus on the late-night hospital sounds coming from the hallway in order to block thoughts about the strong sexual feelings she had felt for Tony, a murderer. She reminded herself that she had thought he was Lieutenant Graham; surely that presumption had colored her feelings. But had it? Finally she fell asleep.

She was awakened in the morning by a new nurse who came in just after the shift change to take her vital signs. "Grace, the night nurse, told me to tell you that your husband—ex-husband, pardon me—was here for about an hour." She stuck the thermometer in Lora's mouth and took hold of her wrist. "But you didn't wake up and he didn't want to wake you. He left some clothes.'' She indicated the chair. ''He told her he had to get back to Selena.''

''Serena,'' Lora said around the thermometer.

''What?''

Lora gestured with her hand that it didn't matter.

The nurse took the thermometer out, then put a blood-pressure cuff around her arm. After she finished, she said, ''Well, dear, your vital signs look good. There's a gentleman outside, waiting to see you. He's apparently been here off and on all night, too.'' She had a twinkle in her eye. She left, and moments later Lora heard a tapping on the doorframe.

''Come in,'' she said, looking toward the open door.

A tall man with blond hair silvering at the temples walked in, and she immediately became aware of the mess her hair was in. Although considering all her contusions, brushing it probably wouldn't have helped much.

''I'm Bill Graham.'' He stuck out his hand, then hesitated. ''You look like you might be too sore to even shake hands.''

She smiled. ''I think maybe I am.'' He looked tired, she noticed, his face drawn. ''You must have been up all night,'' she said.

He rubbed the stubble on his face and nodded. ''I'm so sorry, Lora,'' he said, making another tentative gesture to touch her, then pulling back.

''You couldn't have known.''

''I just shouldn't have taken anything for granted, that the blind date was the man we wanted.''

''I'd forgotten about him. What happened?''

Bill smiled crookedly. ''They sure gave that little guy one helluva surprise. But he was legit. A writer. The name he gave you was one of his pseudonyms. He was apologetic, didn't know why he hadn't given you his real name and was wondering how he would have the nerve to call in with his claim again—using his real name. Or how he would tell you he was Carl Moore, not Thad Morrow or whatever he called himself."

"That was it, Thad Morrow. Nice name."

"Nice guy, but not your type."

"You think you know my type?" she asked with a slight smile.

He shrugged. "I can hope. I met your ex-husband yesterday evening, then again here. He probably would have stayed but I told him I'd take you home. I hope you don't mind."

"No."

"His friend had regained consciousness, he wanted me to tell you, and he needed to get back. He also told me about the assault. I think it was meant for you. Her attacker said your name just before she lost consciousness. That startled your husband when she told him, and then he came to your house. That's where we met."

"What did you think when you got to my house?"

"I didn't know what to think. That maybe we had gotten our wires crossed on where we were going to meet. Then I saw your neighbor and she said you had a date, she thought—that you had left with a man. Then your ex-husband showed up; we got a positive identification from the neighbor, as well as the kind of car he drove from her boy. Turned out the car belonged to a police dispatcher, so he had the license number."

"Lieutenant?"

"Bill."

"Bill," she said, "there was another murder, a coworker of mine—named L.J.—Laura—Andrews. He did it.''

Bill frowned. ''They haven't told me about that. Let me go make a phone call.''

By the time Bill returned, breakfast was being served, so he sat on the edge of her bed and shared it with her.

''You really know how to show a guy a good time,'' he said, spreading jelly on half a slice of toast.

''I'm quite a gourmet entertainer.'' She liked the way his eyes lit up when he smiled.

''Do you know a Brad Conroy?'' Bill asked as he took a bite of his toast.

''Yes,'' she answered, a feeling of revulsion spreading through her.

''He reported that he saw the Andrews woman with a man at a bar shortly before she was killed. Here's the kicker. The same guy had applied for a job at UACA that day. And his address and phone number didn't check out, of course. Conroy gave the police a positive I.D. on Longoria's picture.''

And that's where he got the UACA directory, Lora thought. ''My friend Sue was right. I was the target.''

''Looks like it.''

''It's just hard to believe the man I was with last night killed two people—no, three, including the clerk at that store.''

''Four. You forgot the hit-and-run. A child was killed.''

Lora winced. ''He seemed really nice at first—I mean, I thought he was you.'' She would never mention how attractive he had been to her; that would remain a secret that would gnaw at her for a long time to come.

''Did he tell you he was me?''

She blushed. ''No, he just appeared about the time you

were supposed to and I assumed it was you, so he picked up on it. Besides that, he sounded like you did over the phone—you know, your accent."

He smiled. "I don't have an accent."

She let out a little laugh. "You all sound alike."

"I think *you* all sound alike," he said broadly.

Just then the doctor dropped by, looking at her chart, asked her how she was feeling, and told her he'd release her if she'd take it easy for a day or so. Lora agreed wholeheartedly. After he left, she shoved the tray away, excused herself, and went to the bathroom to change into her own clothes.

"Oh, Lord," she said when she looked at herself in the mirror. Her hair was flat on one side and sticking out at an odd angle on the other. She unsuccessfully tried to fix it, but finally gave up and went back into the room.

56

Tony had driven the Skylark within half a mile of Lora's house, then abandoned it on a suburban street where other cars were parked, and walked the rest of the way. He came in from across the field west of her house, observing that there was no activity in her street, making certain she hadn't gotten home yet. Maybe she was still in that trunk. And maybe the stickup guy would take care of her, if he found her in there. Tony doubted if he would discover her, though. He would probably just abandon the car somewhere.

He slipped a credit card between the jamb and the lock on the back door, opening it easily. Once inside, he was afraid to turn on any lights, but managed to stumble around till he found the refrigerator, opened it, and then found a range-hood light switch. Surely the illumination wasn't bright enough to draw any notice from outside. He washed off in the sink, cleaning the dried blood off his head as well as he could. The rest would have to wait till morning when there would be more light. He went down the dark hall, feeling his way, till he came to a bedroom. He went in and lay down on the bed.

He didn't think he slept, but all at once he was aware of someone coming into the house, a light coming on. He sat up quickly, sending his head spinning with pain. The ache was blinding, but with the light from the hall he managed to get into the corner of the closet. Footsteps came down the hallway, heavy ones, and into the room he was in. The light went on. He knew from subtle things—the sound of the steps, the pace—that it was a man. The man opened a drawer, then another. Tony dared not breathe when something was taken from a hanger in the closet, then a pair of shoes chosen from the ones on the floor. That was it. The man left. Tony heard the steps receding, then the door slammed. He'd left the bedroom light on.

He pulled himself out of the welter of clothes, sweating profusely, breathing heavily. He couldn't sleep now. He went into the dark part of the house, afraid someone might see his shadow, and waited for dawn. It finally came and he could begin to move around the house safely. The waiting still seemed interminable. He made sure nothing showed he was there; he cleaned the sink out thoroughly, switched off the range-hood light, straightened the covers on the bed. He paced through the house. Just as he went into the bathroom, he heard a car pull up. He peeked out the window. Lora was there, accompanied by a man. Shit. Well, he couldn't get back in that closet, not again. The shower curtain was closed; he would get in there.

57

Lora let herself and Bill in and offered to make him a cup of coffee and toast, but he declined. "I'm going to drive downtown and wrap up some details, then I'll come by later. You can get more rest." He started moving to the door.

"I can't tell you how much I appreciate your bringing me home." She hated to see him go.

"I'll be back. Don't worry." He put his finger under her chin gently. "Lora, I'd give you a hug, because I think you need one, but I'm afraid I might hurt you."

She couldn't help it, but tears sprang into her eyes. "Thanks," she said, "I think I could risk it."

He gently put his arms around her and held her close for a few moments, then said, "I want you to rest like the doctor ordered." He glanced at his watch. "How about if I come back at noon and bring some lunch?"

She nodded. Just then the phone rang. He released her and she picked it up. Bill started out the door, but Lora gestured to him to stop when the person on the phone asked for him.

"Graham here," he said into the receiver.

She could only hear the consternation in his voice, but knew it was something serious.

"What is it?" she asked when he finished the conversation.

He sighed deeply, taking her over to a chair and sitting her down. "That wasn't Longoria in the car. God knows what happened. They took the body down to the city morgue and—well, when someone who knew about the case looked at him, he knew right away that he wasn't the right person. He was an eighteen-year-old kid. They haven't got a positive I.D. on him, but it wasn't Longoria."

"That means—that means he's still out there somewhere." Her face registered dismay.

Bill nodded, a worried look on his face.

"And he'll still be after me?"

"I'm going to take you with me, to my brother's in Waxahachie. You'll be safer there. Meanwhile, we can stake out this house."

"I won't argue. Just let me get some things." She went to her bedroom, puzzled momentarily about the light already being on, but then remembered Martin had been there. She dragged out a small overnight case and packed a few things in it—loose things, which wouldn't touch her abused body in any more places than absolutely necessary. She didn't take long and was about to turn off the light, then changed her mind, deciding to leave it on so the house would look inhabited. She stopped in the bathroom to get her toothbrush, which Martin hadn't thought of, and her makeup.

"Do you mind if I call Waxahachie?" Bill shouted to her. "I need to warn my brother's wife that I'm bringing company."

"Please do," she shouted back, and stepped over to the

bathtub, sliding her hand behind the curtain to get her shampoo.

Bill was talking to his brother's wife when she got back to the living room. As soon as he finished, they left the house. She felt relieved when they closed the door behind them, as if the house itself had a hostile presence. It seemed unsafe.

58

As soon as he was sure they had gone, Tony stepped out of the shower. His headache had worsened; he needed to find a painkiller. He rummaged through the medicine cabinet till he found a prescription which said "for pain." He took two tablets and swallowed them by swilling some water directly from the faucet, then went to the living room, sat down and closed his eyes.

He knew he had to get out of there; he'd heard the word stakeout, but what next? With a deep sigh, he opened his eyes, the pain still shooting behind them. He focused on the telephone, then stood up and took a closer look. It had pushbutton dialing and a redial feature. A smile played at his lips; all that time he and a friend had spent as adolescents playing tunes on the phone by dialing various combinations hadn't been in vain.

He pressed the redial, hanging up immediately when it finished dialing. Then he pressed the button again. He did it several times, memorizing the tune, jotting down the corresponding numbers. Then he pressed the redial one more time, letting the call go through.

"Hello?" a woman said.

"Is Janet there?"

"You must have the wrong number."

"Is this the Brown residence?"

"No, Graham," the woman said.

"Is this 555-2914?"

"No, it's 555-2814."

"Sorry," Tony said, hanging up. He carefully corrected the number he had written, then folded the paper and put it in his pocket. Using the number, Tony could find out where the two of them were going. What was it? Waxahachie. But later. Now he needed a cigarette, then he would figure out his next move before a stakeout was set up. He reached for the ashtray on the stereo and remembered Helen Myers, or rather, Helen Myers's empty house. The key lay in the ashtray like an invitation. He could wait there till dark. Then he would just have to make his way back to where he'd left the punk's beat-up car, and set out to find Lora again.

After he finished the cigarette, he went out the back door, in case anyone was looking. One house across the street seemed vacant, but the other one . . . who knows? he thought. Someone might be watching. He went along behind the houses and approached the Myers's house from the opposite side. The neighbor's porch was obscured by ragged, unkempt hedge. Tony unlocked the door and went in. The house was stuffy, so he lifted the windows in the bedroom. The painkiller was making him drowsy, so he lay down and soon fell asleep.

59

"Why? Why does it always happen?" Brenda Graham was muttering as her husband Tom came in the door, two bags of groceries in his arms.

"What?" he asked.

"A wrong number. Just when I've got my hands all full of dough." She held her hands up to show him.

He set the groceries on the counter, then sidled next to her, plucked up a scrap of dough and put it in his mouth. "Pie?"

She nodded. "Cherry. Thanks for going to get those things for me."

"You're welcome. Bill really rates," he said good-naturedly. "You haven't made a pie in a month of Sundays."

"You know why, too. I don't want you to get doughy," she said jokingly, and reached over and pinched his waistline. She made a face at him and put her flour-covered index finger on the end of his nose. "Bill called while you were gone. He's bringing along that woman, the one he came about. I guess she's still in danger."

Tom was putting groceries away. "Do you think there's more to his coming down here than meets the eye?"

She nodded. "Don't you?"

"Uh-huh. It was the way he talked about it yesterday. Did you get hold of Earline?"

"She said she'd try to get someone to take our place at bridge."

"Well, if Bill has this woman here to occupy him, I won't feel so bad if she can't find anyone."

Brenda agreed.

"When will they be here?"

"They're on their way."

Tom found himself anticipating their arrival. He was curious to know what kind of a woman had captured his brother's interest. Especially by phone. He didn't have too long to wait. Bill and Lora pulled up in Brenda's car, which Bill had borrowed that morning.

"Thank you so much for letting me come here to stay," Lora said when Bill had made the introductions.

Tom had to catch himself to keep from staring. The woman before him was bruised and battered, and her hair was hanging lankly around her face.

"Forgive the way I look," she said, as if she noticed astonishment in Tom's expression, her hand going up to her face to cover the bruises.

"You poor thing," Brenda said. "Bill, you need to tell us what in the world has happened." She took Lora's arm and led her to the couch. "Would you like a cup of coffee? I've got a pie in the oven. You can have a piece of that in a little while."

That was Brenda's way, Tom thought, smiling. Food will cure anything. Not that she overate; she simply plied it on others. Except him. She was watching out for his health, she said—a good woman. The phone rang and he excused himself to answer it. It was Earline. She hadn't had any luck finding someone to substitute in their standing bridge game. When Tom got back to the living room, he explained the problem to Bill.

"That's fine, the doctor wants Lora to rest," Bill said, sipping the coffee Brenda had brought him. "We can stay here, watch TV or something. I might run into Dallas this afternoon and see how it's going, but I'll be back this evening so Lora won't be alone."

60

Lora had slept the afternoon away. At twilight, she awoke, unable to figure out where she was. Then, when she tried to turn over and her body contracted in pain, she remembered. She sat up on the edge of the bed, yawning, then got up and went into the living room. Bill was sitting on the couch, reading a magazine.

"Hi," he said when he saw her.

"Hi. I haven't been a very good guest. Have Tom and Brenda already gone?"

"Yes. We didn't want to wake you. Are you hungry?"

She nodded.

"How about pizza? I could go out, pick one up and bring it back here."

"I'd like that. I feel . . ." She gestured to her face, the bruises.

"You look fine; I just thought maybe you'd feel more comfortable not going out."

She nodded in agreement. ''Did you talk to the Dallas police?''

''They haven't had any action at your place. I'll call them again later and see if anything has happened. Meanwhile,'' he rubbed his stomach, ''how about I order the pizza? What kind do you like?''

''Whatever you want, but no anchovies.''

He called in the order. ''I'll run over and get it and be back in a flash. Will you be okay for a few minutes?''

''Sure. I feel very secure here in Waxahachie.'' She smiled to reassure him.

''I'll be right back, then. It's just a couple of blocks down here. Lock the door after me.''

61

''It's supposed to be a deluxe without anchovies,'' Bill said, a little irritated that they had messed up his order when he'd gone to the trouble to call it in so it would be ready.

The boy frowned. ''I'm sorry, sir. We can have another in twenty minutes, and we won't charge you.''

''Okay. Is there a phone?''

''In the vestibule.''

Bill went there and dialed his brother's number.

It rang, but there was no answer. He hung up and dialed again, hoping he had a wrong number. She wouldn't have gone out, he knew. Answer Lora. Answer.

He didn't even tell the boy he was leaving. He just darted out, jumped in his car, and started back to Tom and Brenda's, aware of a sixth sense in him which detected trouble.

Outside the house nothing appeared to be wrong. He let himself in quietly with his key. "Lora?" he said, then repeated it a little louder. He started down the hall, still feeling a sense of foreboding. Then he heard the shower. He pushed the bathroom door open and said, "Lora, are you okay?"

At the sound of a voice, her first reaction was a scream, then: "Migosh, you scared me out of my wits." With wet hair hanging in streamers around her face, she clasped the shower curtain in front of her and looked out at him. "I didn't expect you back so soon."

"I tried to call and no one answered and . . ." He paused, the color rising in his face, and finished simply: "I got scared."

She smiled gently at him. "Thank you, Bill Graham." She leaned over and kissed him, water splashing around them. "Let me finish my shower, then I'll be out."

"I'll call the pizza place and ask them if they deliver. I didn't even tell them I was leaving."

"Maybe we can relax now," he told her as she came from the bedroom, where she'd slipped into slacks and a blue plaid shirt.

"What do you mean?" she asked.

"I called Dallas and they just made an arrest at your house. They're taking him down to headquarters. After we eat, we'll drive back to Dallas for you to identify him."

"Thank God," Lora said with a sigh. "It's over." Bill came over, took her in his arms and held her tightly. He could have stayed there, holding her forever, but the door bell rang.

"Interruptions," he grumbled. "That'll be the pizza."

She laughed. "I'll get us something to drink."

As he unlocked the door, it burst inward. Shots rang out. Bill felt the impact against his body, like a sledgehammer, but no pain. There was just shock and disbelief. Those eyes, those same cold eyes that had stared out of a picture at him. Or was it in an alley somewhere? His thoughts ran together in a microsecond which seemed an eternity. *Lora,* he shouted, *get out of here.* Or did he shout? Maybe he didn't say anything. Maybe he was silent. Things were moving too quickly, spinning, and then there was a void.

62

Lora heard the noise of the door, the almost simultaneous shots, three of them, and came rushing out of the kitchen. She screamed as Bill fell, exposing Tony standing there with a gun in his hand. Something had gone horribly wrong; the police were supposed to have him.

She ran back to the kitchen, horrified by what she had just seen, hoping to escape by the back door. She fumbled with the dead bolt, but before she could get it unlocked, Tony was there.

"Hold it," he hissed through his teeth, "or I'll blow you away, you fucking slitch." He reached over and slapped her across the face.

The sharp blow stunned her momentarily, the fight draining out of her.

"C'mon," Tony said, "We're getting out of here." He motioned which way with his gun.

She went with him back into the living room, where Bill lay on the floor. "I'll go with you, but please let me help him," she begged.

But Tony grabbed her by the arm, squeezing it tightly, and prodded her past Bill and through the front door, with the gun at the small of her back.

They got into a blue VW, with Lora driving and Tony covering her with the gun. She didn't care. She felt desensitized to anything he could do, numbed by the memory of Bill on the floor, maybe needing help.

63

Tony felt high. He had her with him; he had outmaneuvered them, and he had Lora. He would go a little farther, then he was going to stop somewhere secluded and— He felt his fantasies getting the better of him and forced his mind away from them.

He needed sleep; he knew that. Only the adrenaline was keeping him going, even though he had slept for several hours at the Myers's house. Some inner alarm clock had awakened him, and he'd known it was time to get on with things. He had found a can of Vienna sausages in the

Myers's pantry and ate some of them, followed by a mealy apple from the refrigerator. Then he washed down his meal with some Dr Pepper.

Then he had gotten busy. A call to the public library gave him a street address from the Waxahachie crisscross directory; next he needed a state map to find out where in hell this Waxahachie was. He went into the garage and found one in the glove compartment of an old VW Beetle. When he saw the car, and its vintage, he could have shouted. He wouldn't have to walk back to the Skylark. The VW was so old that, if he couldn't find the key somewhere in the house, or hidden in the car, he could hot wire it to get it started.

His search for the key was fruitless, so he rummaged through the garage to find some electrical wire. He cut a piece of it in half, stripped the insulation off the tips, then reached under the dashboard, pulled the ignition and starter wires toward him, and attached his wires to those. He looped the ignition wire over a hot wire, then took the lighter element out and dropped it on the floorboard. The job was done. He stuck the starter wire into the lighter socket. Sparks flew, and the engine turned over and caught. He unhooked his ignition wire and went back into the house to wait until dark.

He saw someone pull up in front of the house across the street, the one with the for-sale sign. The person got out of his car, went into the house, and another man came out, got in the car and drove away. It was probably the stake-out. Soon Tony would lift the garage door, start the VW and back out, and they would be none the wiser.

Then he would get Lora. He sat and imagined her body, its smooth curves, the creaminess of her skin, aware of his growing arousal, pleased by it. He had been disgusted by his reaction to Bart. He went into the bathroom, stripped off his clothes, and dropped them into a heap on the floor. He stood before the mirror, appraising his lean body, stroking himself. Quickly he turned and started the shower, entering its spray.

He had found the Graham house after a stop at a store for directions. He got there just in time to see Bill Graham wheel into the driveway, race up to the porch and go inside. He decided to wait a while and watch. It wasn't long before opportunity presented itself. A delivery truck from a pizza place pulled up in front. Tony was out of his car and over to it in a moment.

"I'll take it in," he had said, fumbling in his pocket apparently for money, but instead pulling out the gun and whacking the kid over the head with it. The boy fell, the pizza with him.

Tony had moved the body up in the shadows next to the truck, then went up to the porch.

And after all his failed plans of the last few days, Lora was now there beside him, smelling fresh as perfumed soap.

He glanced down at the fuel indicator and was alarmed to see that it hadn't moved since he left Dallas. All he needed was to run out of gas on the interstate. His eyes scanned the roadside for a gas station.

64

Jack Turner was humiliated. And it was all that damn Doris's fault, this compulsion of his. If she had ever been there when he'd needed her, he wouldn't have resorted to other means of satisfaction, wouldn't be on his way to police headquarters, handcuffed like a common criminal. With a heavy sigh signaling resignation, he slumped down deeper into the seat of the squad car.

Back in the early sixties, when he and Doris had just been married a year or so, she was already holding out on him. An old horny dame had lived next door, and Jack had discovered he could get off by watching the woman when he saw her undressing from his window. Jack was sure she undressed at that window for his benefit. Then Doris had gone and planted a bush in front of the window, for privacy, she said. But he remembered the smug little smile on her face as she said it. He couldn't very well protest too much.

Sometime in the ensuing years window peeping had become a habit. He could get satisfied and there was the feeling of danger. No matter where they lived, he had found someone to watch. The watching was never too risky, but it felt dangerous, like he was living on the edge. Some guys jumped out of airplanes, others climbed mountains, and he looked in other people's windows.

The last time, Doris had really nailed him, caught him in the act of peeping, and she had used it as an excuse to throw him out, blackmail him, really. He hàd decided then that he'd better quit, and he'd succeeded until Lora moved in across the street. He'd controlled his compulsion until the other night.

Then he had looked out tonight and had seen that one light in her window. He had left his house quietly; the interior lights and the porch light were off so as not to silhouette his body. The lights were on in several houses down the street, but the street itself was dark. Several cars sat in driveways, one car parked next to the curb two doors down, but no one was stirring. He felt like the only person alive, really charged up. Her window beckoned.

If he was silent, they were more so. He didn't hear them till they told him to freeze. What a nightmare. And it was just beginning.

65

He is going to win, Lora thought. It's incredible. After all this, he is going to win. It's just a matter of time.

She was very tired, too tired to be driving. Perhaps it would be easiest just to allow herself to fall asleep at the wheel. An accident would take care of him, so he couldn't go on killing people. But she didn't like that idea; he needed to suffer. That thought gave her a little burst of energy.

They were driving down the interstate toward Waco. "Pull into that service station," Tony ordered.

Lora obeyed, leaving the multilaned highway, stopping at the county road that crossed it, then pulling into the station and up to the self-service pumps.

"Now, I'm going to get out, and I want you to crawl across the car and get out on my side," he said. He opened the door and put his legs out but stayed halfway in the car while he grabbed her by the arm and pressured her across the seat.

Awkwardly she got her legs across the gear shift, then pulled herself over to his side, getting out right behind him. He kept his hand in his pocket on the gun. He stayed right beside her as she got the nozzle and pulled the lever down to start it pumping.

Lora glanced up at him. He was watching her carefully for a false move. She looked over at the office of the station and could see the man inside, standing behind the counter, waiting for them to come in to pay. Another man came from behind the right side of the station as if to go inside. Incredibly, it was Bill Graham. Lora blinked then looked back at Tony, who was watching her. She paid attention to pumping the gas—she mustn't alert Tony—but her mind was racing. Bill wasn't dead; that thought made her heart lift. He had somehow followed them. He was here. She resisted the urge to look back over at him.

The automatic nozzle clicked off. Lora pulled it out, holding it with both hands, turned to put it back on its hook, but as she swept it around, she pulled the trigger like a gun, dousing Tony with gasoline.

"Damn you," he shouted at her as she dropped the nozzle and ran. She saw Bill Graham level off with his gun just as a car came between him and the VW, blocking his way. As Lora ran around beside the station, she heard Bill shout to the people in the car, trying to warn them. She reached the restroom and turned the knob, thinking it would be a place to stay safely out of the way, then noticed the sign that said, ASK FOR KEY.

66

Tony instinctively jumped back into the VW to escape. He hadn't seen Bill Graham at first, but when the car between them peeled out, he saw him there, leveling the pistol at him. Christ, he wished he had some ammunition for the gun.

The smell of the gasoline permeated his nostrils, making him woozy. That goddamn woman, he thought, realizing that somehow there was respect for her wrapped up in his comdemnation. She was no wimp. He reached down and jammed the starter wire into the lighter. He didn't even see the spark.

67

Bill and Lora were just finishing breakfast, a Mexican omelet she had prepared.

"And she can cook," he remarked. "That's a whole lot better than hospital food."

"Thanks." She smiled at him.

He glanced at his watch. "I hate to say it, but I guess it's time for me to be getting to the airport." His one-week furlough would be up tomorrow and he would be back to the grind.

They drove to the airport silently, each caught up in his and her own thoughts.

"Martin called yesterday," she said, breaking the silence. "Serena gets out of the hospital tomorrow and they're going to go down and apply for a marriage license."

Bill nodded. "How do you feel about that?"

"A little funny. I mean, it really closes one whole part of my life."

"That's how I felt when Marianne remarried. But it frees you, too—you'll see."

"I suppose." She knew what he meant. She already felt different—maybe because all that had happened this week had put her in touch with her own mortality—and morality, she thought with a smile. One thing she had discovered about herself was that she was a fighter. And that felt good to know.

They drove on in silence.

"I've really enjoyed this week . . . well, except the first couple of days," Bill said. "It would have been better if I hadn't been laid up, of course." He grinned mischievously at her.

"I just thank God you weren't wounded more seriously."

"Me, too. I'm just lucky it was a low-intensity round and didn't hit a vital organ. Christ. He was at point-blank range, and if he'd had any other kind of a gun—well, I wouldn't just have a hole in my side and a broken rib to worry about. I wouldn't have *any* worries, come to think of it." He paused for a moment, then continued, "Actually, had it been a better gun, that guy in the convenience store would have probably killed Longoria then and there, and the rest wouldn't have happened." This was about the hundredth time they had gone over the week's events, but Lora wondered how many more such discussions they would have before she'd feel purged of the shock.

"I'll never get over hearing that explosion, then coming around that corner and seeing you lying there, flat on your back. I thought you were dead—for the second time that night."

"Frankly, I thought maybe I was a goner when it blew me off my feet."

She shuddered, and Bill reached over, gently pulling her hair away from her forehead. "It's over."

"Yes," she said. "I guess so."

EPILOGUE

''Claims, Lora speaking.''

''I'd like to file a claim on a missing person in my life.'' Lora's heart lifted. A month had passed, and she hadn't heard a word from him. At the airport they had agreed to wait and see how they felt during the next few weeks, before contacting each other again.

''Bill?'' she said tentatively.

''Would you go out to dinner with me?''

''What?''

''Go out to dinner with me. I've made the reservations for tomorrow night.''

''You mean, in New York?''

''There's a ticket for you at the American counter at DFW. Will you come? It'll be a real date.''

''Yes,'' she said, then more enthusiastically, ''Yes, of course, I'll come.''

''And I'll be waiting,'' Bill said.

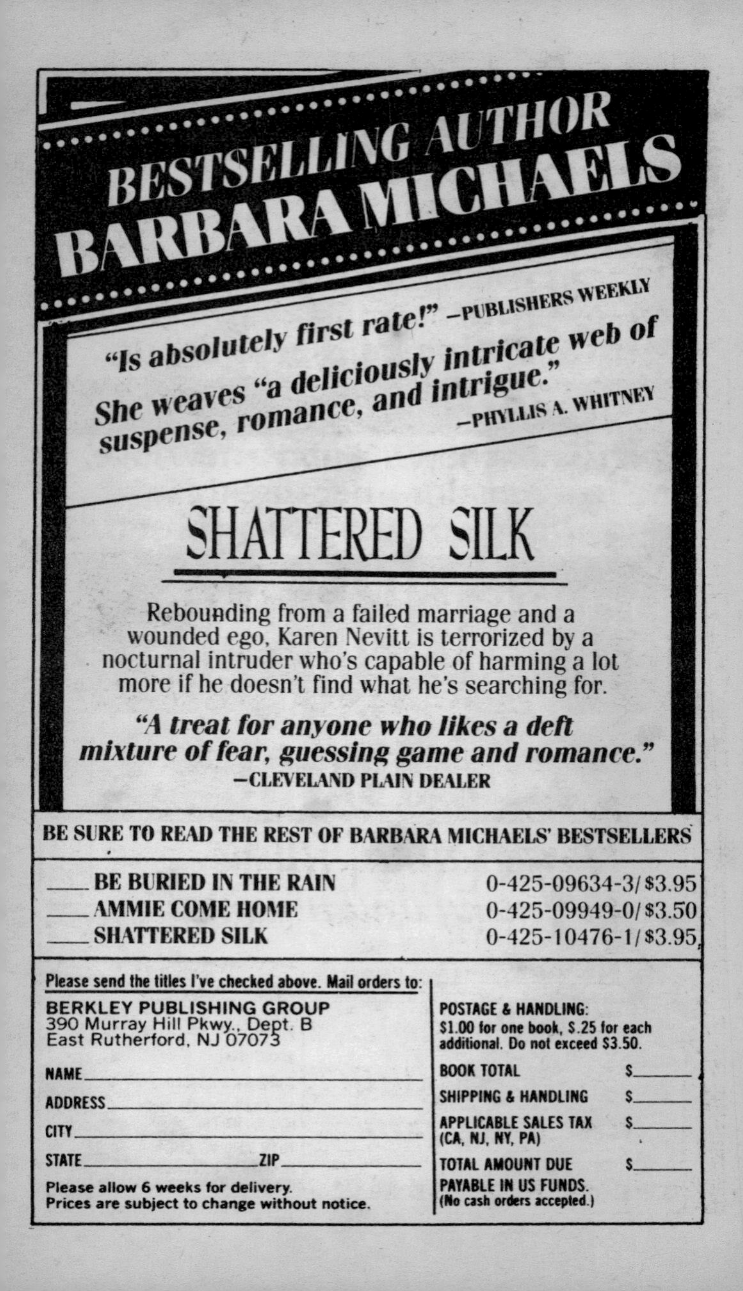

BESTSELLING AUTHOR
BARBARA MICHAELS
"Is absolutely first rate!" —PUBLISHERS WEEKLY
She weaves "a deliciously intricate web of suspense, romance, and intrigue."
—PHYLLIS A. WHITNEY
SHATTERED SILK
Rebounding from a failed marriage and a wounded ego, Karen Nevitt is terrorized by a nocturnal intruder who's capable of harming a lot more if he doesn't find what he's searching for.
"A treat for anyone who likes a deft mixture of fear, guessing game and romance."
—CLEVELAND PLAIN DEALER
BE SURE TO READ THE REST OF BARBARA MICHAELS' BESTSELLERS
____ BE BURIED IN THE RAIN 0-425-09634-3/$3.95
____ AMMIE COME HOME 0-425-09949-0/$3.50
____ SHATTERED SILK 0-425-10476-1/$3.95
Please send the titles I've checked above. Mail orders to:
BERKLEY PUBLISHING GROUP
390 Murray Hill Pkwy., Dept. B
East Rutherford, NJ 07073
NAME
ADDRESS
CITY
STATE ZIP
Please allow 6 weeks for delivery.
Prices are subject to change without notice.
POSTAGE & HANDLING:
$1.00 for one book, $.25 for each additional. Do not exceed $3.50.
BOOK TOTAL $
SHIPPING & HANDLING $
APPLICABLE SALES TAX (CA, NJ, NY, PA) $
TOTAL AMOUNT DUE $
PAYABLE IN US FUNDS.
(No cash orders accepted.)

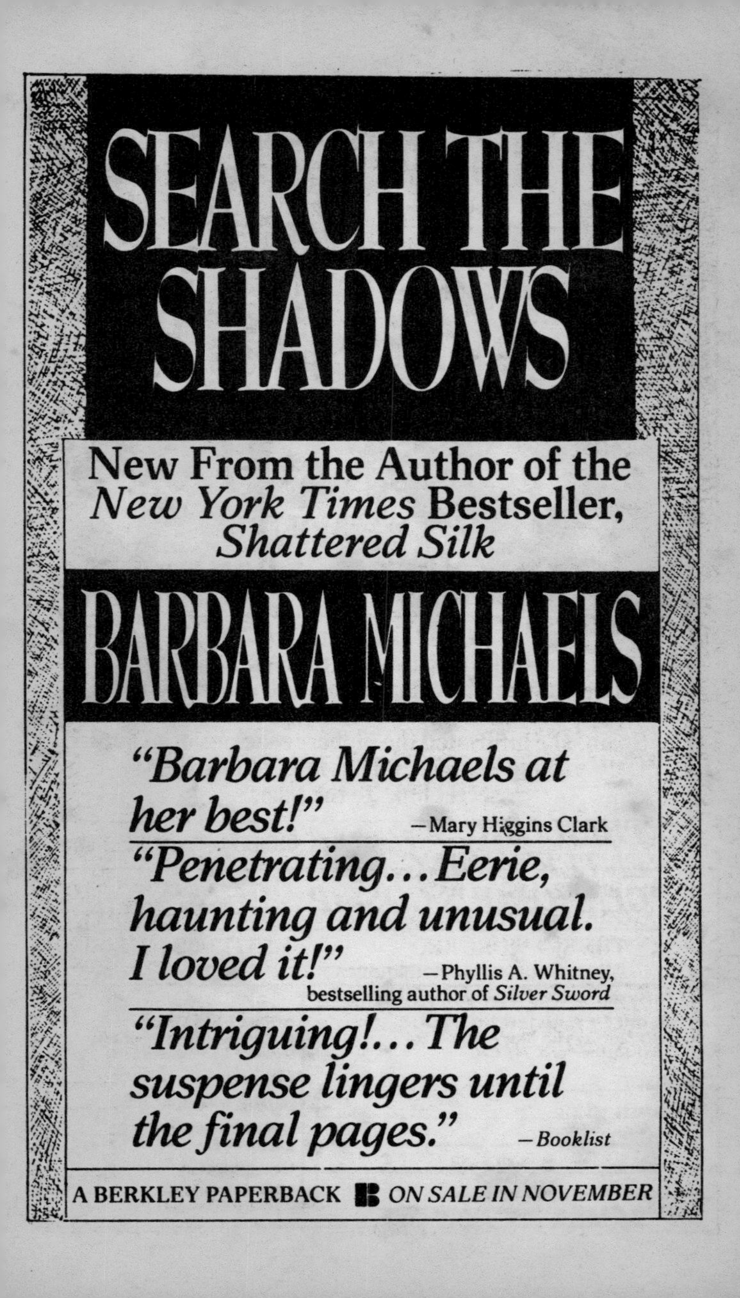
SEARCH THE SHADOWS
New From the Author of the
New York Times Bestseller,
Shattered Silk
BARBARA MICHAELS
"Barbara Michaels at her best!" —Mary Higgins Clark
"Penetrating...Eerie, haunting and unusual. I loved it!" —Phyllis A. Whitney, bestselling author of Silver Sword
"Intriguing!...The suspense lingers until the final pages." —Booklist
A BERKLEY PAPERBACK
ON SALE IN NOVEMBER